DOLPHIN ISLAND

Shipwreck

Read all the books in the *Dolphin Island* series:

Jenny Oldfield

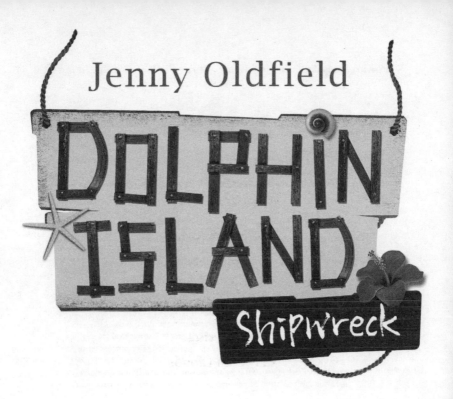

DOLPHIN ISLAND
Shipwreck

Illustrations by
Daniel Howarth

Hodder
Children's
Books

For lovely Lola, Jude and Evan – three dedicated dolphin fans

HODDER CHILDREN'S BOOKS

First published in Great Britain in 2018 by Hodder and Stoughton

1 3 5 7 9 10 8 6 4 2

Text copyright © Jenny Oldfield, 2018

Inside illustrations copyright © Daniel Howarth, 2018

The moral rights of the author and illustrator have been asserted.

A CIP catalogue record for this book is available from the British Library.

ISBN 978 1 444 92827 3

Typeset in ITC Caslon 224

Printed and bound in Great Britain by Clays Ltd, St Ives plc

The paper and board used in this book are made from wood
from responsible sources.

MIX
Paper from
responsible sources
FSC® C104740

Hodder Children's Books
An imprint of Hachette Children's Group
Part of Hodder and Stoughton
Carmelite House
50 Victoria Embankment
London EC4Y 0DZ

An Hachette UK Company
www.hachette.co.uk

www.hachettechildrens.co.uk

Chapter One

'Oh no!' Mia Fisher sat cross-legged on the deck of *Merlin*, her family's yacht, as they sailed smoothly through deep blue water. She had dropped one end of a seashell necklace she was making for her big sister, Fleur.

Fleur heard the shells skitter-scatter across the wooden deck of the bathing platform and looked up from her book. 'Oops!' she grinned.

'Help me pick them up,' Mia pleaded. The sun was scorching hot on her back and the breeze blew wisps of dark brown hair across her cheeks as she scrambled to gather the tiny, spilled cowries.

'What's this doing down in the galley?' Their brother, Alfie, popped his head up through a hatch. He held a reel of nylon fishing line that had rolled from

Mia's lap as she'd jumped up to rescue her shells.

The boat, set fair for an evening passage between small, rocky islands in the South Pacific, dipped and rose again. The white sails billowed in the wind.

Fleur took the reel from Alfie. 'What's for tea?' she asked.

'Dad's cooking sausages.' Deciding to give Mia a hand, Alfie came up the companionway dressed in red shorts and trainers. After four weeks under the tropical sun, his fair hair was bleached pale blond and his wiry body was tanned.

'What's Mum doing?' Closing her book on butterflies, thirteen-year-old Fleur stretched on her sunlounger, adjusted her pink swimsuit straps and yawned.

'She's plotting our course for tomorrow and checking for echolocation images of hidden reefs.'

'It's a wonder you're not working that out with her.' Fleur liked to make fun of her techie brother's love for touch-screens and numbers. At eleven years old, Alfie knew his way around echo-sounders and electric compasses better than anyone else on board. Personally, she preferred butterflies and birds – in fact, any beautiful creature that she'd discovered flying, crawling, climbing or scampering along white beaches and through thick jungle on the hundreds of tiny islands scattered like green jewels across the azure sea.

'Isn't *anybody* going to help me?' Mia wailed. She was hungry, hot and only six. And the necklace was ruined.

'Don't whinge,' Alfie said, down on his hands and knees to pick up shells. 'We can soon make another.'

'Yes, there'll be millions of shells on the next beach – don't you worry.' Fleur shaded her eyes with her hand and looked at the frothy wake that the boat made in the clear water. 'Wow – look!' she exclaimed, pointing at a pod of twelve or so bottle-nose dolphins that had risen to the surface to play in the white foam.

The smooth, glistening creatures leaped clear of the water with a volley of whistles and shrieks that made Fleur, Alfie and Mia clap their hands and laugh out loud. The dolphins twisted and turned their torpedo-shaped bodies in the air, rolled and dived then appeared again. Some slapped their tails against the surface of the sea, others swam close to the boat, heads above the water, mouths curled upwards in broad smiles and blowing raspberries at the excited spectators.

'Cute!' Fleur sighed.

'I like this one best.' Alfie pointed to the nearest dolphin, which was smaller and smilier than the rest. 'She's young and she's all pink and pearly underneath.' He leaned over the rail for a better view. 'I wish I could swim like that. I'm useless in the water.'

'Which is why you should be wearing this.' Their mother, Katie Fisher, had appeared on the bathing platform with three life vests. 'Put it on, please, Alfie. And you too, girls.'

Grumbling, Alfie, Fleur and Mia did as they were told while the dolphins went on playing. Two other youngsters showed off by rising straight out of the water and doing what the kids called tail-walking – flapping their front flippers against their sides and doing a comedy walk with their tail flukes. The petite, pink pearly one surged ahead to ride the bow wave at the front of the boat.

'Don't you just love them?' James Fisher, the children's father, was the last to appear on deck. He

looked funny with his bare chest and cooking apron tied around his middle over his denim shorts. 'Anyway, tea's ready,' he announced.

So Mia, Alfie and Fleur tore themselves away from the sight of dolphins at play and went below deck to put on T-shirts, trainers and shorts ready for tea. They listened, as they ate, to their mum and dad arranging to take turns at the wheel overnight to steer them through some narrow straits ahead.

'We're in uncharted waters,' Katie warned. 'Lots of these islands don't even have names and there are hidden reefs everywhere.'

'Don't worry – we're used to tricky situations after four weeks' non-stop sailing in these waters.' James sounded relaxed as he ran a hand through his dark, curly hair. 'And your granddad made sure that *Merlin* has the best navigation equipment that money can buy.'

The Fishers had borrowed the 46-foot yacht from Katie's wealthy father for six weeks of tropical sailing during the summer holidays. They'd flown out from grey old England to Queensland, Australia, then kitted *Merlin* out with all the provisions they would need for a long sea voyage and set off across the Torres Strait towards Papua New Guinea. They'd laid anchor in many a sheltered bay and explored empty white beaches fringed with palm trees. It was proving to be the adventure of a lifetime, a dream come true for all the family.

'Yes, we definitely owe my dad a big thank you!' Katie knew how lucky they were. With her fair hair permanently tied back and her tanned, round face displaying a wide, white smile, she too was confident of sailing safely through. 'Come on, Alfie – if you've finished your sausages I'll show you our exact course.'

'And we'll do the hard work.' James hauled the girls back up on deck to stow away the mainsail. 'We're old hands at this,' he joked.

As they worked together, Mia kept a hopeful lookout for dolphins while Fleur, whose hair fell about her face in auburn curls, pictured the moment when she could play her usual sunset game of standing at *Merlin*'s bow, staring out to sea and pretending to be the heroine in a romantic film.

When they were almost done, Alfie came up the

companionway to report a problem. 'Mum's lost the signal. The screens have gone blank.'

'Yeah, the satellite link is pretty weak out here.' James sighed. 'Tell her not to worry. We can rely on the manual compass and old-fashioned maps for the time being.'

Meanwhile Fleur had taken up position at the bow of the boat. 'Dad, I can see dark clouds,' she said uneasily. 'Does that mean a storm's heading our way?'

James came up beside her in the fading light and studied the eastern horizon. 'They didn't mention it in the forecast, but yes – it looks like we'd better be prepared.'

'Maybe atmospheric disturbance is the reason we lost the signal.' As usual, Alfie's techie knowledge came in handy. 'I'll go and tell Mum.'

'I don't like storms,' Mia moaned. 'They make the sea rough and I feel sick.'

'Nobody likes them,' Fleur explained. She felt sorry for Mia and took charge of taking her down below, leaving their dad to switch on the engine and keep an eye on the approaching storm.

'We definitely didn't expect this.' Sitting at the chart table with Alfie, Katie struggled to bring the network system back to life. A wind had got up, and they felt the boat begin to dip, rise and dip again as the sea grew choppy.

'I'd better rescue my sunlounger,' Fleur decided, nipping back up on deck in time to see the flimsy canvas bed caught by a gust of wind. It skittered across the platform, making her gasp as it was blown like a kite over the stern guard before flapping off into the sunset. She saw her dad in the cabin, looking serious, with his hands gripping the wheel as *Merlin*'s bow rose to meet a giant wave. Up they went, with a sickening lurch, up and up into a wall of green water until they crested the wave then plunged back down.

'Fleur!' Katie's anxious voice called from the navigation station. 'Come back below deck!'

'Ouch!' The downward plunge had pushed Fleur off balance and thrown her against a steel guardrail. She bent forwards and was fighting her way back towards the companionway when the next wave hit. Up the boat rose again, with the sound of the wind whipping and whistling through the rigging and with water slapping hard against the hull. To keep upright, Fleur grabbed the nearest thing – a bracket securing the life-raft canister to the deck. She held on tight as a heavy spray drenched her, but was so shocked by the strength of the wind that she hardly dared to look up at the whirling mass of dark cloud and mist about to envelop them.

'Come down!' Katie called again.

Fleur let go of the bracket and scrambled to safety before the next wave hit.

'What's it like up there?' Alfie wanted to know.

'Pretty bad,' she admitted. 'It's starting to rain. I'm sorry, Mum – we lost the lounger. The wind blew it overboard.'

Hearing this, and with strict instructions for the kids to stay below, Katie hurried to check the situation for herself and consult with James.

'It's getting really dark all of a sudden.' Fleur shivered. Her skin felt cold and prickly from the salt. 'The waves are giant and we're tiny in comparison. A little white speck in a massive sea.'

'Sshh – you'll scare Mia,' Alfie warned.

All three sat at the chart table staring at blank screens and holding tight as *Merlin* rose and fell then rose and fell again. They listened to the thud of water against her sides, waiting for their mum to come back.

'OK, listen to me,' Katie said when she returned, her fair hair soaked and plastered to her head. Her face was deadly serious. 'It looks like there's a typhoon coming up from the south-east.'

'Is that one of those curly-whirly things?' Mia whimpered, edging closer to Fleur and putting both arms around her waist.

Alfie frowned but said nothing.

'Dad's doing his best to work out its exact position,' Katie explained quickly. 'He needs to know wind speeds and directions and that's harder to do without our systems up and running. Alfie, you can keep on trying to pick up a signal. Fleur, you look after Mia. I'll be up there with Dad.'

'I don't like this. I want it to stop.' Mia's eyes filled with tears as she clung to Fleur.

Alfie concentrated on the empty screens. 'I wish we had reception.' He tapped keyboards and adjusted an aerial. 'At this rate the storm will throw us off course and we won't have a clue where we are.'

'Now who's scaring Mia?' As the boat rolled from side to side then rose up into another huge swell of water, a howling wind drowned Fleur's voice and once more they all had to cling on to something solid – the table or the navigator's seat – whatever was closest.

'How are you doing down there?' their dad yelled from above. He'd handed over the wheel to Katie and was battening down hatches but the wind buffeted him so badly that he had to crouch and hang on to the steel guard wires. Rain lashed his face and he could scarcely catch his breath.

'We're OK,' Fleur called back as *Merlin* lurched and rolled.

Then suddenly – disaster! There was a loud thud then a churning, scraping noise from the stern of the boat – the sound of the propeller blades hitting something big and solid, followed by a high whine from the engine in the compartment under the companionway.

'What in God's name was that?' James struggled

against the wind to reach the stern, only to find that they'd been hit full-on by a long, dark object – most probably a tree trunk that had been felled by a previous storm and pushed out to sea. From what he could make out, it had mangled the propeller completely. 'Cut the engine!' he yelled at Katie, before he was tossed forward by the swelling waves then thrown back painfully against a metal mooring cleat.

'Dad!' Alfie left the navigation station and climbed the companionway to see James sprawled across the deck. Katie stood helpless at the wheel as the storm drove *Merlin* close to rocks that had appeared through the mist to starboard. Then at the last second the current snatched the boat away and sent her wildly in the opposite direction through foaming water towards open sea.

'I'm OK,' James said, ignoring the pain in his ribs as he crawled forward to join Katie.

'We're drifting!' she yelled. 'Without a propeller there's nothing we can do – except ride out the storm and hope we're still in one piece when it's over.'

'I'm scared,' Mia whimpered, still clinging to Fleur,

who steadied herself against the back of the navigator's seat and braced her legs against the chart table. 'How long will it last?'

'Not long,' Fleur assured her, though the boat was being tossed like a cork and the wind howled louder than ever.

'Dad – we're losing the life-raft!' Alfie spotted the latest threat and made as if to scramble up on deck. 'It's coming loose from its bracket!'

'Stay where you are!' James yelled. The wind whipped his words away and his attention was taken by the sight of more pyramids of jagged rock looming up ahead.

Ignoring the order, Alfie made a desperate attempt to save the life-raft canister. He hauled himself up on deck and with one hand still gripping the companionway rail he reached towards it. His fingers made contact with a loose strap then a wave hit them from the side and the boat tipped violently to starboard. Alfie lost hold of the rail and was sent skidding on his belly backwards towards the bathing platform, scrambling for a fresh hold as heavy spray engulfed him.

Down below, Fleur held Mia tight. She'd seen Alfie's skinny legs disappear up the companionway and her heart thudded in her chest. 'Don't be stupid, Alfie – come back!' she cried.

Tossed by the waves and sucked hither and thither by the current, *Merlin* once more scraped past fingers of dark rock and bobbed on aimlessly. The mist was thick, the sky almost black in the centre of the storm.

Alfie lay spread-eagled on the smooth bathing platform. The life-raft canister had broken free and was gone so his efforts had been in vain and now there was nothing to grab on to except the stern guard. But it was too high for him to reach and he felt himself slide again. For a split second *Merlin* steadied and almost gave Alfie enough time to rise to his knees and hold on to the guardrail but then another wave hit the stern full on and she tipped upwards to an angle of sixty degrees. Again Alfie was thrown back and this time he was flipped free of the boat. He fell through thin air, through mist and spray into the foaming sea.

Chapter Two

Merlin rose. Up and up she went as the wave rolled on. Below deck, Mia and Fleur felt but couldn't see the force of water and wind.

The boat crested the wave and plunged downwards on Nature's terrifying rollercoaster. From the cabin, Katie and James saw nothing but spray. A wall of wind deafened them and made their senses spin so that they didn't hear their iron keel slice into the rocks submerged just centimetres below the surface – only felt *Merlin* come to a shuddering halt then rock violently from side to side as she caught fast on jagged rocks.

Below deck, Mia screamed. Fleur saw seawater rush in through a hole low in the hull. It swirled in and rose quickly and her first thought was to look for something to stem the flow – she tried a cushion from the bench-seat but water was pouring in too fast for her to stop it so all she could do instead was to grab Mia and drag her up the companionway. 'Whatever you do, don't let go of my hand!' she cried as she poked her head out of the hatch. 'Mum, Dad, Alfie – where are you?'

There was no reply. *Merlin* had settled sideways on to the rocks and water still poured in through the glass fibre hull. On deck, the door of the cabin hung open but there was no one inside. And there was no sign of Mum, Dad or Alfie either.

'Where is everyone?' Mia wailed. Her pretty face with its delicate features was screwed up in an agony of fear.

'It's OK, we're wearing life vests and the clouds are lifting – I think I caught a glimpse of land out there.' Fleur wasn't sure, but the waves seemed to be lessening and the wind dying down. She began to hope that the worst of the storm had passed. One thing was sure though – they had to get off the boat before it finally keeled over and sank. 'Hold on to me,' she urged Mia as they edged their way on deck. 'And listen – I can definitely see land through the mist. It's not far away.

We're going to try and reach it – OK?'

'Will we have to swim?' Terrified to go anywhere without her mum, dad and Alfie, Mia pulled back.

'Yes. Hold on to me.' The boat lurched and tipped. The bathing platform was already below water. In the low light of the setting sun Fleur saw that trying to reach land was the only choice they had.

But the waves were strong and they were weak. A thirteen-year-old girl and her six-year-old sister – what chance did they have against the tail-end of a typhoon? With her heart in her mouth, Fleur hesitated. Then she saw something miraculous.

One shape, then a second, rose from the water – sleek grey creatures with domed heads and curved fins. They leaped clear of the waves and through the mist, re-entered the water then emerged again – two young dolphin rescuers. They swam so close to the rocking, sinking boat that Fleur could reach out and touch them. She looked into their dark, bright eyes and knew in an instant that they were here to help.

'They want us to join them in the water,' Fleur whispered to Mia. 'Don't be scared. Ready?'

Mia nodded. She too trusted the dolphins.

So, with no more time to think, the sisters held hands, took deep breaths and jumped. They plunged into the foaming sea away from the stricken boat and let the two young dolphins swim alongside. The dolphins opened their mouths and gave friendly low yelps and small clicking, chattering sounds, quickly coming alongside to offer their front flippers to Mia and Fleur.

'We have to grab on to them,' Fleur realized. She persuaded Mia to hold on to the flipper of the nearest dolphin, who held steady while his companion waited for Fleur to do the same.

'Don't leave me,' Mia pleaded as Fleur's dolphin surged ahead with Fleur in tow. The words were hardly out of her mouth before her own rescuer followed suit.

The girls felt the dolphins' speed and power. They rushed through the water towards land, which gradually emerged through low clouds – a white beach fringed by windswept palm trees, backed by dark, vertical rocks with a forested hillside beyond.

'Hold on tight!' Fleur yelled at Mia. She felt the tug

of a strong current below the surface and was glad that she had secure hold of the dolphin's flipper.

Next to Fleur and her dolphin, Mia closed her eyes and held on. Salty spray washed over her face and the waves kept on breaking over her.

At last the dolphins reached the shore then waited for Fleur and Mia to loosen their grip. The girls let go of their flippers and found their feet – they felt soft sand beneath them and the gentle lap of water against their legs.

'Thank you!' Fleur breathed a huge sigh of relief. She reached out to take Mia's hand. The two dolphins stayed in the shallow water, watching as the girls waded on to the beach.

'Where are we? Where are Mum and Dad?' Mia's voice was small and frightened. 'Where's Alfie?'

Fleur shook her head. Wind swept across the beach from the east as the sun sank over a rocky headland to the west. There were no footsteps in the smooth sand – not a single sign that any living creature was here. She crouched beside Mia and wrapped her arms around her. 'I don't know where they are,' she sighed. 'But you and me – we're here together and we're safe.'

*

In the eye of the storm, Alfie had been flung from the boat. He hit the water and sank, closing his eyes and holding his breath until he thought his lungs would burst. Then his life vest bobbed him back to the surface. He gasped and lunged towards *Merlin*, who was on her side and letting in water fast. His fingertips almost touched her smooth white hull but the strong current swept him away amongst flotsam from the stricken boat – plastic bottles, cushions, a fire extinguisher and coils of rope. Alfie kept his head clear of the water and tried in vain to swim back to her.

It was no good. Though he kicked with all his might, he made no progress. In fact, it was the opposite – the current was dragging him further and further away from *Merlin*. The sea foamed and swirled. Alfie cried out for help.

His call was answered. A dolphin appeared out of nowhere, her nose nudging him gently away from the boat into a thick mist. She had a small head and a pink belly and the curve of her mouth made her look as if she was smiling at Alfie and telling him not to be afraid.

'You!' he gasped. 'You're the pearl dolphin.'

The dolphin nudged him again and ducked underneath, soon rising to let him take hold of her curved dorsal fin, so he could sit piggyback fashion astride her broad body.

Hope rose inside Alfie's chest. His pearl-pink dolphin would keep him safe and head for the nearest shore. All he had to do was to cling on.

And sure enough, with a flick of her strong tail she swam through the dying storm and clear of fatal currents, between black volcanic rocks and above coral reefs with a sure sense of direction until Alfie, riding on her back, could see a way ahead.

There was a wide bay with a beach. There were palm trees and dark rocky headlands ... and two small figures standing hand in hand, looking out to sea.

*

'Alfie!' Mia saw him first. He was sitting astride the smiley dolphin from earlier. 'Look, Fleur!'

Fleur let go of Mia's hand and ran into the sea, calling Alfie's name. She held her arms above her head and waved.

The young dolphin came close to the shore then stopped. 'Thank you,' Alfie murmured as he slid from her back and splashed down on to his hands and knees. 'You saved my life.' Then he felt Fleur's hands pull him to his feet.

'You made it!' she cried, hugging him tight then leading him to dry land.

Her job done, Alfie's pearl dolphin turned back out to sea. Then with a flick of her forked tail flukes she was gone.

'Where are we?' He took in the beach, the leaning palms and black cliffs.

'We could be anywhere – we have no idea.'

'What happened to Mum and Dad?'

Fleur shook her head and hid her fears from the others. 'We don't know that either. But try not to worry – the dolphins will help them too.'

'Are we stranded?' Alfie wanted to know. His legs felt weak and his whole body battered by the waves.

The only answer came from white gulls rising into the pink sky from the headland to the west. They soared high and their raucous calls split the air.

Fleur shrugged and shook her head. All she knew for sure was that the wind was dying down, the clouds lifting and that the three of them had survived the shipwreck. She also realized that before long the sun would set. 'Listen, Alfie – we don't have much time before it gets dark. We have to try and make some sort of shelter.'

Mia stood at the shoreline, waiting for Alfie and Fleur to come back. She saw coconuts bobbing in the shallow water and stooped to pick one up but quickly dropped it again when a crab scuttled out from under a nearby rock. She ran back to dry land.

'You're right – it might rain again during the night.' Alfie took a quick look around. 'Maybe we could use palm leaves. There are plenty lying about.'

Fleur nodded and took charge. 'Mia, we're going to make a shelter. Over there, by those rocks – I can see a cave. We'll need as many palm leaves as we can find – some to put on the floor for us to lie on, some to prop against the entrance to stop the wind blowing in. Come on – we have to be quick.'

More gulls rose from the rocks as the three Fisher children drew near, dragging palm leaves through the sand. The rocks cast long shadows over the beach. The red sun sank low in the sky. Out to sea, about half a mile from the shore, *Merlin* leaned further on to her side. As her steel mast buckled and her mainsail unfurled, her hull shifted then settled again on the rocks.

'Hurry!' Fleur lined the cave with palm leaves while Alfie and Mia propped them against the entrance. They didn't have time to be scared or to worry about what had happened to their mum and dad. All that mattered was to keep safe and dry. 'Good, we're doing great. We'll need more leaves over here, on this ledge. This can be a bed for you, Mia. Alfie, you can sleep over there. I'll stay awake and keep a lookout.'

In the background, the sound of waves crashing on to the shore and the whoosh of wind through the palm trees reminded them of their narrow escape but they were too busy to notice the small pod of dolphins patrolling the bay, still keeping careful watch over the three young castaways.

*

The shelter was finished just before sunset. The wind had died down and bats flitted noiselessly from tiny crevices in the cave where Fleur, Alfie and Mia had taken refuge, escaping into the black night.

Fear rose again in the silence. It began with a knot in the children's stomachs, twisting and rising, knocking at their ribs, mounting to their throats and resting there like a hard lump that made it difficult to swallow.

'I wish I had Monkey with me,' Mia said in a small voice. Monkey was her favourite soft toy. She always took him to bed to help her get to sleep. 'And I want Mum and Dad to come,' she whimpered from her ledge.

'We all do,' Alfie said with a shiver. He couldn't bear to think what might have happened to them. And who knew what was here in the cave with them besides bats? Spiders as big as your hand and creepy-crawlies, scorpions and snakes – they could all be lying in wait, ready to pounce.

As Fleur sat in the doorway watching the full moon rise high in the sky, she felt tears well up. She did her best to hide them for Mia's sake, but Alfie spotted them and crept close. He sat down beside her and without saying anything he took hold of her hand. Together they gazed at *Merlin*'s upturned hull shining white in the moonlight. Millions of stars twinkled.

'Try to sleep,' Fleur told Alfie and Mia. 'In the morning we'll decide what to do next.'

Chapter Three

Shortly after sunrise next morning a small gecko woke Alfie from his shallow sleep. It ran down his bare arm then sat on a ledge as still as a miniature statue, staring at him with bulging, lizard eyes.

'Hey, get away from me!' Alfie swatted at it with the back of his hand.

'Why did you do that?' Fleur asked. 'He hasn't done anything to you.'

With a flick of its tail, the pale green gecko scuttled along the ledge towards the opening of the cave where Fleur had spent the night. Then it ran down the vertical rock and sat down beside her, staring out to sea.

'You're cute,' she murmured.

'I'm cold. I'm hungry. I'm thirsty,' were Mia's first words when she opened her eyes. Her mouth was so dry and sore that it was hard for her to swallow.

'Coconut milk,' Alfie said abruptly as an idea struck him. 'Wait here.' He ran without explanation out of the cave on to the cool white sand, scooped up the nearest coconut then started to bash it against a rock.

'Alfie's right. There's milk inside. We can drink that.' Drained from staying awake all night looking out for Katie and James, Fleur sat and watched Alfie crack open the large round shell.

'Uh-oh!' A hard thump from Alfie had split the coconut wide open, letting the whitish liquid spill on to the sand. 'Not to worry – we can eat the inside bit instead.' Prising the moist, sweet flesh from the shell, he handed some to Fleur then to Mia who nibbled at it before deciding she liked the taste. She sucked it hard then went on to take bigger bites.

'Want some?' Fleur asked her patient little gecko friend who squatted beside her looking out to sea. Between bites of coconut she struck up a conversation with him. 'Can you see our dolphins? Three of them rescued us during the typhoon. They were really brave.'

The gecko opened his mouth and flicked out his

incredibly long, insect-catching tongue to lick the small piece of coconut she'd placed in front of him.

'Dolphins are amazing, aren't they?' Fleur went on. 'They're not doing anything exciting right now – just swimming around keeping an eye on us. But you should see them when they jump out of the water and spin in midair. It's fantastic!'

With a mouth full of coconut, Alfie cocked his head to one side. 'He's a gecko. He can't understand you – you do know that, don't you?'

Fleur tossed her long hair back from her face. 'We're not listening, are we, George?'

'George!' Alfie echoed.

The gecko jerked his head towards her and stared.

'See – he even knows his name!' George was cool, Fleur decided. He'd let them share his cave for the night and was now happy to hang around for a chat. For a few seconds he even let her forget the fact that their mum and dad were still missing. It was only when Mia surprised him by suddenly jumping down from her ledge that her new green friend took fright and scuttled off across the beach.

Mia sidled up to Fleur. 'Are we still lost?' she asked in a mournful voice.

Fleur looked at her sister's forlorn face. 'Yes, but wait till Mum and Dad find us – they'll be able to work out where we are.'

'You hope,' Alfie muttered behind her back. He strode down to the shoreline in search of empty plastic bottles, cans and cartons amongst the wide band of seaweed and driftwood washed up by the storm – anything that might come in useful if it turned out they were stuck here for ages. It was best to keep busy, he thought, and not think bad things.

'When?' Mia pleaded. 'When will they work that out?'

'Soon.' Fleur hoped she sounded more confident than she felt. She told herself that their parents had been thrown overboard during the storm, just like Alfie, and that friendly dolphins had been there to guide them safely ashore. 'They could be in the bay next to this one, past those rocks where the sun's coming up.'

'Look what I found!' Alfie raced up the beach carrying two plastic bottles complete with tops and a long length of fishing line tangled in seaweed. 'These are going to be dead useful.'

'Smelly.' Mia turned up her nose at the rotting seaweed.

'Yeah but we can carry on making that shell necklace with the line,' Fleur promised.

'Or catch fish with it,' Alfie pointed out. His blond hair was spiky from dried seawater and his brown arms and legs were covered in sand.

'That sounds cool,' Mia agreed. She felt the warmth of the rising sun on her chilly limbs and let a smile creep across her face as, out at sea, Alfie's pearl dolphin led the pod in an early morning game of chase across the width of the glittering bay.

'If you're going to call your gecko George, I'll call my dolphin Pearl,' Alfie decided.

'And mine is Stormy.' Mia easily picked out the dark grey shape amongst his paler grey friends. She recognized his white belly as he leaped clear of the sea.

'Mine's Jazz,' Fleur decided. She knew him because his mouth turned down at the corners more than the others and he had dark shading around his eyes. Right now he was tail-walking and waggling his front flippers as if he were dancing.

Pearl, Stormy and Jazz – everyone agreed they were good names. In fact they were so busy enjoying their dolphins that they missed the sight of two figures slowly cresting the headland to the west and staring down in amazement on to their beach.

*

'Thank God!' Katie stood beside James on the windswept rock. They saw Fleur, Alfie and Mia on the white sand watching dolphins play in the bay. 'They're safe,' she whispered.

James took a deep breath then remembered that his side hurt from when he'd fallen against the mooring cleat. He suspected that he'd cracked at least one rib and if so, it would take a while to heal. 'Safe,' he echoed gently.

He and Katie had been swept by a giant wave out of *Merlin*'s cabin, overboard into the ocean. They'd been dragged underwater in a maelstrom of bubbles and pulled by a strong current away from the coral reef then pushed back up to the surface so far away from the boat that there was no hope of them being able to swim back to rescue Fleur, Alfie and Mia. The storm had them in its grip and they'd been tossed and tumbled mercilessly by the waves. Soon they'd lost sight of the boat and had to struggle to stay afloat. James had swallowed salt water and been blinded by spray. Katie had closed her eyes and prayed. Neither had expected to survive.

But the typhoon had been short and sharp – it had blown itself out as suddenly as it had begun. Then a warm current had caught hold of Katie and James and driven their battered bodies on shore, casting them up on to a beach in a narrow cove where, just before nightfall, they'd gasped and crawled their way out of the water. They'd spent the dark hours huddled together under the nearest palm tree, waiting in a fog of fear for the sun to rise.

At the crack of dawn in the east, Katie and James decided on a plan of action.

'We were all wearing life vests,' Katie recalled. 'There's every chance that, even if the kids were washed overboard like us, they managed to stay afloat.'

James had to believe that this was true. 'But where are they now?' he wondered as two adult bottle-nose dolphins approached the shallows of their cove. Their curved fins cut through the blue water towards them. Almost beaching themselves, they lifted their tail flukes in the air and sent out a volley of clicks, creaks and deafening whistles to draw the worried parents' attention.

'What are they trying to tell us?' Katie ran into the water as if expecting the dolphins to talk.

Unable to follow because of the agonizing pain in his ribs, James watched closely. 'Look – they're swimming back towards the headland.'

'And now they're turning and coming back to us again!' Losing her footing in a hasty attempt to follow them, Katie slipped under the water and emerged gasping.

'Do you think they want us to make our way into the next bay?' James wondered. 'Is that what they're saying?'

'Yes – and this is the quickest route.' Excited clicks and squeaks from their dolphin guides accompanied

Katie's efforts to scale the nearest rocks. Slowly James joined her, doing his best to ignore the sharp pain in his side. Together they reached a place that gave them a view of the neighbouring beach.

It stretched out in a shallow white curve edged by a fringe of white foam and a broad expanse of azure sea. Katie and James saw the upturned wreck of *Merlin* half a mile out and then, as their gaze swept back towards the beach – a miracle – three small figures watching a pod of dolphins at play.

'Thank God!' Katie whispered.

Their two dolphin guides rolled belly-up in the water, clapped their flippers against their sides, then swam away to join the others.

*

Down in the bay, Mia, Alfie and Fleur caught sight of two figures outlined against the bright light above the cliff. They were hazy and shimmering and Fleur thought they must be a dream, so she stood rooted to the spot. Alfie closed his eyes and opened them again to make sure they were real.

'Mum!' Mia sank in the soft sand, stumbled forward

on to both knees then picked herself up and began to run.

Racing after Mia, Alfie and Fleur gasped as their mum fell and scraped her legs on the rough volcanic surface, but she didn't seem to care.

'Alfie!' Katie cried, landing at last on the soft sand and running towards them. 'Fleur! Mia!'

The children felt their hearts would burst with joy.

Their dad too made it on to the beach. He fell to one knee, got up, then stumbled towards them.

Mia flung herself at Katie. Her mum's arms were around her and her dad was staggering over to Fleur and Alfie.

'You made it!' James said over and over. One arm was around Alfie's shoulder, the other around Fleur's waist. 'We all did! Can you believe it – we came through a typhoon. We're alive!'

Chapter Four

'Nobody knows we're here, do they?' As usual Mia spoke what was on everyone's minds. 'How will anybody find us if they don't know where we are?'

There was a long silence then Alfie jumped in with a solution. 'We have to make them see us. I know – we'll build a fire!'

Fleur liked this idea. 'Planes will fly over us – they'll be able to spot a fire, especially at night.'

'And sailors,' Alfie added. 'They're bound to pass by sooner or later.'

'The fire comes later,' James argued. 'First we need to find out more about where we've washed up, thanks to those amazing dolphins.' He scanned the beach then spotted the cave that the kids had used as their overnight shelter. 'What was it like spending the night in there?' he asked.

'Scary,' Mia admitted. 'It was dark and smelly. And the seagulls kept me awake.'

'There were hundreds of bats and loads of spiders in there.' Alfie shuddered.

'Any snakes or scorpions?' Katie asked.

'No but there was a gecko,' Fleur said. 'He's called George.'

'Trust you!' Katie said with a grin. 'But I'm thinking we should build a new shelter further away from the sea where it's not so windy.'

'And away from these flies.' For the first time Alfie noticed that the sand was alive with tiny hopping insects. He felt a sharp nip each time they landed on his skin and he noticed that his legs were already covered in small red bumps.

'So, James – you and the kids will go inland to find a spot for us all to hunker down while I climb those rocks to get a better idea of where we are.' Katie pointed to the cliff that rose almost vertically behind the palm trees. 'I'll find out if we're on an island and, if so, how big it is then report back before the sun gets too hot.'

'And look out for any sign of fresh water while you're up there,' James suggested.

Alfie spoke for Fleur and Mia. 'Yes, please – we're thirsty!'

'OK, gang – let's go.' If James was worried he didn't show it. Instead he walked slowly up the beach, bending awkwardly to collect palm leaves as he went.

'We need to find a shady spot under the trees,' Fleur pointed out as she overtook her dad.

'Wait for me!' Mia cried, seizing the nearest palm leaf and dragging it along. It was bigger than her and left a trail in the soft sand.

Alfie followed in their wake with his two plastic bottles and tangled fishing line while Fleur detoured to their cave to collect their life vests and check in on George. 'See – we're moving out already,' she told the gecko when she found him sitting on one of the vests. 'But don't worry – I'll come back and visit once we've built our new place.'

George flicked his tail. When Fleur picked up the yellow vest he didn't scamper off but stayed exactly where he was.

'Are you coming too?' she asked.

He twitched his scaly green head to one side then scuttled along her arm up on to her shoulder.

'Cool!' Fleur grinned. Then she and George left the cave and hurried after the others.

*

'This should do,' Fleur said.

They'd chosen a shady spot encircled by palm trees with a thicket of low, broad-leaved shrubs to either side and a semicircle of large, smooth boulders behind. The beach spread out before them with a view of *Merlin* wrecked on the rocks. The sea sparkled under a clear blue sky.

While she, her dad and Alfie settled on the best spot for their new shelter, Mia stood on the beach gazing out into the bay and sighing loudly.

'What's up?' Alfie laid his precious bottles on the grass then looked out to sea with her.

'The dolphins have gone.'

'So what? They're probably fishing.'

'Will they come back?' Mia missed seeing Stormy in

the calm water. She felt safer when he was there.

'Maybe.' Alfie couldn't say for sure but he hoped so. After all, he owed his life to Pearl.

'Hey, you two – you're meant to be helping us!' Fleur called. While they'd been busy talking, their dad had showed her how to start their shelter by bending saplings to form a roof. Now he'd gone back down the beach to collect more palm leaves. 'I need rocks to anchor the ends.'

It was hard, thirsty work to lug stones heavy enough to keep the saplings in place and soon all three were sweating in the heat. But when James returned with leaves to make a thatch he was pleased by what he saw.

'Good job!' he said. 'It's starting to look like home – once we make the roof watertight we can take a rest.'

They worked on, using anything they could find to fix the palm fronds in place. Alfie went to the shore and brought back a length of frayed rope that he'd spotted earlier while Mia and Fleur spied creepers looping through the bushes. They tore them down and found they could be used like twine.

'It's OK for you,' Fleur told George, who was

watching with interest from a sunny boulder. 'You can sleep anywhere.'

Two hours later, with the shelter almost finished, James was satisfied that there would be room for them all to sleep. Coarse grass growing underfoot gave a soft surface for them to lie on and all in all he was pleased with what they'd done.

'Here's Mum!' Mia called. She'd stepped out of their new home to see if the dolphins had come back but instead she spotted Katie making her way down from the cliffs.

'Do you want the good news first or the bad news?' she asked them, her face shiny with sweat and her fair hair plastered to her head after her hard climb.

'Bad,' James said quietly.

'This is definitely an island and there's no one else on it,' she reported. 'I could see from end to end when I was up there. I reckon it's about two miles long and half a mile wide, covered in tropical forest and fringed all around with beaches and rocky coves but not a hut or a shack in sight.'

'I can't say I'm surprised,' James said with a

heavy sigh.

'The good news is – there's fresh water! I spotted a spring bubbling up from deep underground. It turns into a stream then a waterfall – not too far away from here.'

'That's cool.' Alfie breathed a sigh of relief then produced his two empty bottles. 'We can fill these up.'

'No sooner said than done,' Katie agreed and, without more ado, the two of them set off to collect the precious water that would keep them alive.

*

'Now we have something to drink and somewhere to live.' James smiled at Fleur and Mia after they'd put finishing touches to their roof then sat cross-legged on the floor of their new shelter. 'That's not bad for Day 1.'

'And dolphins!' Mia said brightly, pointing out to sea.

To the delight of Mia and Fleur, Pearl, Stormy and Jazz were back in the bay with the rest of their pod. A dozen curved fins cut through calm blue water; heads and smooth grey backs bobbed above the surface, circling the wreck of the Fishers' boat. One dolphin slapped his tail against the water, another rose to rest his belly against the upturned hull of the boat. They

45

joined together in a chorus of high whistles, inviting Fleur and Mia down to the water.

Though they were tired from building their shelter, the girls sprang to their feet and waved at the dolphins as they ran to the shore.

'Hi, Jazz, hi, Stormy!' they called, clapping their hands and waving.

It was Pearl who leaped clear of the water – once, twice, then three times. She twisted in the air and plunged out of sight in a mass of foaming bubbles, then emerged to whistle out a greeting.

'Hi, Pearl!' Alfie raced down the beach to join his sisters. He and Katie had brought fresh water back with them. 'It's me – Alfie!' he yelled to his dolphin. 'This island is cool. We've built a shelter. We've got water. All we have to do now is find something besides coconuts to eat!'

*

'Fire next?' Alfie suggested.

The sun was sinking in the west and the sky turned soft pink. Everyone was tired and hungry, lost in their own thoughts as they gathered outside the entrance to their shelter.

'You're right, Alfie,' James agreed. 'Before we eat we have to make sure we can keep warm when the sun goes down. But making a fire here on a desert island isn't easy.'

'No matches.' Never one to waste words, Alfie put his finger on the problem.

'Exactly.' Fleur took his point and recalled what she'd seen on a TV programme about castaways. 'Don't we have to rub two sticks together to create a spark?'

'Yes. It's the friction that does it.' Planning ahead, Alfie scrabbled eagerly in the undergrowth for handfuls of dry grass. 'This can be our kindling, along with some twigs,' he explained. 'Mia and Fleur, you can fetch driftwood from the beach.'

James agreed, saying that he and Katie would search the shrubs bordering their shelter.

So Fleur and Mia set off with a spring on their steps. 'I remember what to do,' Fleur said confidently. 'You have to rub the sticks for ages then all of a sudden the spark sets fire to the grass.'

'Will this do for firewood?' Mia picked up an old

plank that was almost hidden under dry seaweed and shells. It had arrived on a high tide, along with a rusty metal grate that might also be useful.

'Perfect.' Fleur meanwhile had spotted another hefty piece of driftwood – a branch stripped bare of its bark and whitened by the sun.

For a while they scoured the beach, then went back to base, lugging with them the grate plus anything that would burn.

'This time yesterday was when the typhoon hit,' Katie reminded everyone. Taking two sticks, she got ready to rub them together.

'This is guaranteed to make your wrists ache,' James predicted. 'You'll have to rub for ages before you can create enough friction to make a spark.'

'You're right.' Katie took a deep breath then cast a sad glance out to sea to where *Merlin* lay on her side. 'Back then we had a beautiful sloop-rigged boat in full working order and a network system with all mod cons. Who would've believed that twenty-four hours later we'd be cast away on a desert island and living like cavemen?'

'Stop talking, Mum – just do it.' Alfie crouched with his hands cupped around the dried grass.

'OK. As soon as you see a spark, blow gently to make the straw catch light.'

Fleur, Mia and James held their breaths as Katie and Alfie began work.

'It's taking for ever,' Fleur groaned, aware that George had perched himself on a nearby rock to get a good view of the fire-lighting activities. 'Don't even ask!' she told him with a sigh.

The gecko sat still as a statue and stared.

'Patience,' James murmured.

Mia kept her fingers crossed and watched intently.

'There!' Katie cried as the first red spark fell.

Alfie pursed his lips and blew, then his heart sank as the spark faded and died.

'Never mind. Keep going,' Fleur urged.

'Again!' Katie watched the second spark fall.

This time Alfie blew and the spark turned into a tiny yellow and blue flame.

'Careful. Gently does it.' James saw the flame flare and fade then flare again. Soon the dried grass was well ablaze and Alfie laid small sticks in a pyramid over it, fanning the flames and waiting with bated breath to hear the crackle of burning wood. Sure enough, the kindling caught alight and they could relax.

'Excellent!' Fleur said, but George didn't agree. At the first sight of the flames he'd fled from his rock into the bushes.

'Now for the big stuff.' Katie decided it was time to add heavier wood. She placed small branches carefully over the kindling then stood back to watch the flames lick at them.

'If only we had some fish to cook.' Alfie's stomach rumbled at the thought of food.

'And a pan to fry them in, and some oil. Oh, and a barbeque with beef burgers, sausages and steak!' Fleur dreamed of the impossible.

'Fire is a good start,' their dad insisted. 'And coconuts will have to do as supper for tonight.'

'Yuck – coconuts!' Mia pulled a face.

'This morning you said you liked them,' Fleur reminded her.

'Not all the time.' Suddenly Mia was distracted by

dolphins in the bay and she cheered up in an instant. 'Can we go swimming?' she asked.

Katie nodded. 'Your dad and I will stay here and keep an eye on the fire. We can't run the risk of it going out now that we've got it started.'

'Don't go too far out of your depth. Watch for currents!' James's warnings followed Mia, Alfie and Fleur down the beach to the water's edge.

'Dolphins, here we come!' Mia yelled. A wave lapped her ankles then sucked sand from under her feet before she took off her T-shirt and plunged full-length into the next wave.

'Come and play with us.' Fleur was already waist-deep when Jazz rose into the air for pure joy, plunged underwater then resurfaced right beside her. 'Brilliant! Come into the water, Alfie – everything's fine.'

Alfie hesitated. He remembered the moment when yesterday's giant wave had crashed into him and flipped him out of the boat – the nightmare feeling of being dragged down and tossed like a rag doll this way and that.

Then he saw Pearl waiting for him. She was smiling,

with only her head and curved fin above the water, looking at him with dark, kind eyes. In the background, other dolphins rode the waves, vanished and came up again to play. 'Here I come!' he called to Pearl in a shaky voice, as he braced himself to wade into the next wave. He panicked as it broke at shoulder height and swept him off his feet. Under the surface he went and then up again, to where his trusty dolphin waited for him. With a sigh of relief he flung his arms around her and laid his head against her wet, velvety flank.

Chapter Five

At last the Fishers' first day on the island came to an end.

The children swam with the dolphins then went back to their new home, guided by smoke from the fire that rose through the tree canopy into the evening sky.

'Do we have to have coconut for supper?' Mia pestered her dad, knowing full well what the answer would be.

'Sorry but yes,' came the steady reply. 'How would you like it, everyone – fresh out of its shell or toasted over the fire?'

'Hmmm.' Fleur considered her answer as if she was studying the menu in a posh restaurant. 'How about cooked for a change?'

'Char-grilled it is!' Her dad grinned and laid out

pieces of white flesh on the wire grate they'd rescued from the beach. He pushed it into the hot embers and soon the smell of singed coconut filled the air.

'Well?' he asked after he'd pulled their dinner out of the fire and served it on a glossy green leaf. 'How is it?'

'Perfect!' Fleur giggled as she chewed.

'Yucky!' Alfie and Mia chorused.

'Better than nothing,' Katie added stoically.

The kids ate as much coconut as they could, drank plenty of water, then made their way into the new shelter while their injured dad rested under the palm trees and their mum once more went off in search of firewood.

Alfie chose a spot furthest away from the entrance then settled down for a good night's sleep.

Mia checked the floor for creepy-crawlies then lay down beside him. 'This grass tickles,' she complained, but the words were hardly out of her mouth before she fell fast asleep.

Fleur decided to lie close to the entrance where she would be able to see the sky. 'Look, George – there are millions of stars up there,' she whispered to her faithful

gecko. Millions of stars and an endless ocean whose waves crashed against the rocky headlands and lapped at their empty beach. She went to sleep thinking about the infinite black space between the stars and didn't wake until the sun crept up over the eastern horizon.

*

'Day 2!' Alfie announced as he stepped outside the shelter, spread his arms wide and turned his face towards the rising sun. 'Hey, Mia – what do you say we make a calendar?'

'What for?' was the sleepy reply from inside.

'To record how long we stay on the island,' he explained.

A tousle-haired Mia emerged into the sunshine. 'How?' she asked.

'We find a long stick then we mark it with charcoal from the fire – one line for every day.' Alfie thought rapidly as he made for the undergrowth at the foot of the cliff. 'It's not high-tech but at least it'll mean we can keep track of the time.'

Careful not to burn her fingers, Fleur, who was already awake, extracted a burned twig from the fire that had been kept going overnight by their mum and dad. 'Ta-dah – charcoal!'

Alfie returned with a long stick. He began to press one end into the ground outside the shelter then had second thoughts and took it inside. 'It's best to put it in a dry place – the charcoal will smudge in the rain,' he predicted.

Fleur handed the burned twig to Mia. 'Start at the bottom,' she suggested. 'Make two marks – one for yesterday, one for today.'

Proudly Mia made the first marks on their calendar then stood back to admire her work.

'Mum and Dad said for us to fetch more water before breakfast,' Fleur told Alfie and Mia. 'They went off along the beach to collect firewood. We'll follow you, Alfie.'

Happy to take charge, he picked up the two water bottles and led the way to the base of the cliff. 'It's steep,' he warned Fleur and Mia, 'but it's safe if you follow me.'

'Easy-peasy!' Mia insisted. She scrambled effortlessly up the rock, eager to reach the top.

But Fleur climbed more slowly. She took in the

glossy green plants growing in crevices and speckled brown spiders spinning webs between their broad leaves. 'Wow!' she exclaimed, pointing to a trumpet-shaped scarlet flower that was blowing in the breeze – a sort that she'd never seen before. A bee buzzed past her face then alighted on one of the brilliant red petals. It collected pollen then buzzed on to the next flower. 'And, wow – look at this!' This time it was an amazing butterfly basking in the sun that drew Fleur's attention. It was deep blue, as bright as any jewel, with black spots on its delicate wings, and when she put her hand close beside it she saw it was the size of her open palm. 'I wish I still had my butterfly book, then I could find out what it's called,' she murmured.

'Come on, Fleur – stop saying wow and get a move on!' Alfie yelled from the top of the cliff. His loud voice roused a flock of small red and green parrots from the palm trees on the beach. They squawked crossly and flapped up into the air then flew out of sight. 'At this rate we'll die of thirst.'

Reluctantly Fleur left her sapphire butterfly and climbed on to find Alfie and Mia already crouched by

58

the side of a stream that ran between bare rocks. She could hear the rush of water tumbling over a nearby ledge and Mia's sighs of delight as she dipped her toes in. Alfie meanwhile scooped water between his palms then took long gulps.

'Just think – no one's ever been here before.' The idea thrilled Fleur as she too sat on a rock and dangled her feet in the water. The place was humming with wildlife – long-legged flies floated in a pool to the far side of the stream and a small blue bird with a long orange beak hovered nearby. 'We're the first people ever to drink here in the whole history of the world.'

'We don't know that for sure,' Alfie said, splashing water over himself then shaking his head like a dog when it emerges from a river. 'This land could have been attached to the mainland – ages ago in the time of dinosaurs. Then, the ice age came along and after the ice melted sea levels rose. That's when this place turned into an island.'

'But that wouldn't mean people were here, clever clogs! It would be diplodocus and tyrannosaurus.' Mia the dinosaur expert put Alfie right for once.

Bickering and splashing water at each other, Fleur, Alfie and Mia forgot they were here to fill the bottles until a distant shout from down on the beach reminded them.

'Hey, you three!' James yelled, pressing one arm against his injured ribs and waving with the other to attract their attention. 'It's breakfast time.'

'Yummy!' Alfie frowned at the idea of more coconut.

'Race you back,' Mia told Fleur. She started to pick her own way down the cliff. 'I bet my way's better than yours.'

Meanwhile, Alfie filled a bottle and handed it to Fleur. 'Don't worry about Mia – she'll be OK. She'll meet us back at the shelter.'

So Fleur and Alfie set off the way they'd come, soon losing sight of their little sister.

'It's just like her to go wandering off,' Fleur grumbled. 'If she has an accident we're in dead trouble.'

'She won't,' Alfie predicted. 'You know what Mia's like on the climbing walls back home – she scrambles up and down like a monkey.'

But when Alfie and Fleur reached the bottom of the

cliff and there was no sign of Mia, even Alfie began to worry.

'Don't tell me you let her go off on her own,' James groaned when they reached base.

'You stay here and rest. The rest of us had better go and find her,' Katie sighed. She strode on to the beach from where she could get a good view of the cliff, followed by Fleur and Alfie.

Katie shaded her eyes and scanned the dark rock and the forest beyond. 'Mia's turquoise T-shirt shouldn't be too hard to spot.'

'There's the waterfall, splashing down over those rocks. That's where she set off from – just above there.' Alfie pinpointed the spot.

'But no sign of her,' Katie sighed.

There was a long, worried silence.

But then, lo and behold, Mia made them all jump. She sprang out from behind a rock, her shoulders draped in a dripping piece of white fabric that she wore like a superhero cape. 'Look what I found!' she cried, running across the beach towards them.

'Where on earth have you been?' 'What is it?'

'Where did you find it?' The questions rained down thick and fast.

'I found it in a rock pool over there.' Mia seemed surprised that her game of hide and seek had misfired.

'Here, let me see that.' Alfie took the improvised cape from her and showed it to the others. 'I don't know about you but I reckon this came from *Merlin*.'

'You're right – it's a piece of sail and it doesn't look as if it's been lying around for too long,' Fleur agreed. 'The mainsail must have got ripped apart during the storm and this part of it washed up on last night's tide.'

'It could come in useful,' Katie muttered. 'Good girl, Mia – all is forgiven. But no more wandering off by yourself – OK?'

With a cheeky grin Mia promised then nabbed the cloak back from Alfie. She put it round her shoulders and zoomed off to the water's edge.

Sighing with relief, Katie prepared to report back to James. 'Go and tell Supergirl that breakfast will soon be ready,' she told Fleur and Alfie. 'And this time don't let her out of your sight.'

*

'Rule number one – always stay together. Never split up.' Mia's solo adventure had led Katie and James to lay down the law as the family sat in the shelter after a morning beachcombing for firewood.

'Rule two – don't eat anything you don't recognize even if it looks delicious. It might be poisonous. Rule three – drink plenty of water. And rule number four – stay out of the midday sun.' This meant that Fleur, Alfie and Mia were forced to take a siesta during the hottest part of the day.

But staying out of the sun and doing nothing made Fleur fidgety. 'Can we figure out how to weave sunhats?' she wondered, picking up a palm frond and twisting it between her fingers.

'Cool!' Straight away Alfie took up the idea and got to work. He quickly worked out that he could use a length of salvaged rope as a headband. 'Like this – you make a loop and tie a knot then you weave the fronds in and out, like in a basket.'

It was a method that seemed to work and soon he, Mia and Fleur had made rough headgear to protect themselves from the sun.

'High fashion!' Fleur giggled as she jammed it on her head.

'Why not weave mats while we're at it?' Alfie suggested. 'Then we can lie on them at night.'

Again they started eagerly, but when they found that mats took longer than hats they quickly grew bored.

Mia was the first to give up and wander outside, dressed in her cape and new hat. 'I spy with my little eye …' she began, her eyes twinkling with excitement.

'Something beginning with D?' Alfie asked when he and Fleur joined her at the edge of the beach.

'Yes – dolphins!' she cried.

They were back – Pearl, Stormy and Jazz, recognizable in an instant, but quietly keeping their distance about a hundred metres out to sea. The kids counted eight dolphins altogether then speculated on why the pod had formed a tight semicircle at the eastern side of the bay.

'Why aren't they playing games and making us laugh?' Mia asked.

'Maybe they're asleep,' Fleur suggested.

'With their eyes open?' Alfie wondered.

Fleur presented them with an impressive dolphin fact that she'd read in one of her sea life books. 'They sleep with one eye open. One side of their brain goes to sleep but the other stays awake.'

'That's cool.' Alfie was intrigued. 'I know they use echolocation to find their way around. That's pretty cool too. And they pick up really high noises that humans can't hear.'

'So why aren't they playing?' Mia said again. She walked ahead of the others across the hot sand to the lapping shoreline.

The dolphins didn't react. They kept to their semicircle even when Fleur, Mia and Alfie waded into the sea.

'Did you see that?' It was Alfie who spotted a small silver fish leap clear of the shallow water then vanish.

'And another.' Fleur saw a second silver flash. In fact, when you looked closely there were dozens if not hundreds of fish swimming around their ankles, each about twenty centimetres long, darting this way and that as Pearl and her dolphins slowly began to close in on them.

'It looks like the dolphins are fishing for their supper,' Alfie guessed.

'They're working as a team, herding the fish towards the shore.' Fleur watched Jazz and another dolphin dive below the surface and come up with fish clenched between their jaws which they then swallowed in one gulp. 'Clever!' she murmured.

The determined pod swam closer until, driven to the very edge of the sea, a multitude of silver fish flipped and flopped at the children's feet.

'They're not just fishing for *their* supper!' Alfie realized with a sudden thrill. 'They're doing it for us too!'

'You're right!' Almost without thinking, Fleur snatched the piece of sailcloth from Mia's shoulders. 'Take a corner each,' she instructed the others. 'This is our fishing net – ready, steady, scoop!'

Together Fleur, Alfie and Mia dipped the cloth into the shallow water while the dolphins corralled the helpless fish. The children hauled it out again to find seven or eight plump, gleaming fish twitching and turning in the makeshift net.

'Thank you, thank you!' Mia clapped her hands and laughed. Stormy raised himself out of the water and flapped his flippers against his side. With a loud chirp and a whistle he plunged back into the sea.

'How cool is that!' Alfie could hardly believe their luck.

Pearl bobbed out of sight then reappeared with a splash of her tail flukes. Taking this as a sign that their job was done, the other members of the pod broke the semicircle and pursued their own catches, knowing that there were fish galore for dolphins and their landlubber friends.

'Yummy-scrummy!' Mia declared, racing ahead of Alfie and Fleur to announce their surprise catch.

Chapter Six

Grilled fish had never tasted so good. The soft white flesh fell away from the bones and melted in the mouth and a gulp of spring water washed it down perfectly.

'Happy now?' Katie asked Mia, who sat cross-legged inside the shelter, licking her fingers clean.

Mia nodded happily.

'Good, because it's time for you three to go and fetch more wood,' James decided.

'Do we have to?' Fleur protested. She felt lazy after their first proper meal on the island and anyway she was more interested in finding out about the parrots they'd spotted when they'd been fetching water from the spring. Her guess was that they lived high in the branches of the palm trees that formed the canopy above their shelter and were none too pleased to have their island peace shattered by five noisy castaways.

'Yes – this fire doesn't feed itself,' her dad insisted as he shooed them on to the beach. 'It's a full-time job to keep it alight.'

Reluctantly following orders, Alfie, Fleur and Mia made their way towards the bat cave where they'd spent their first night.

'There was a whole load of old branches and logs stuck in there,' Alfie reminded the girls.

'We'll drag them out and pile them up at the entrance before we start carrying them back,' Fleur decided. It felt creepy going from bright sun into deep shade until her eyes got used to the dark and she saw George perched on his usual ledge, his tiny feet splayed and his flat head cocked to one side. 'Don't worry,' she told him. 'We're here to collect firewood then we'll leave you in peace.'

 Who says I'm worried? he seemed to ask, watching with interest as Mia lugged the first piece of driftwood out of the cave.

It was hard, hot work and of course it wasn't long before Mia lost interest and wandered off across the beach, idly picking up shells and taking them down to the water's edge to rinse them clean.

'Ignore her,' Alfie told Fleur as he dragged a heavy branch out of the cave. 'Even Mia can't get into trouble collecting shells.'

'Want to bet?' Fleur said, watching Mia wade knee-deep. She was too busy with her shells to notice a wave come rolling in. 'Whoops!' Fleur cried as the wave broke and swept Mia off her feet.

Together Fleur and Alfie charged to the rescue, running into the sea to drag a dripping Mia clear of the water.

But Mia wriggled free, sat down and let another wave wash over her. 'This is fun!' she cried.

'Mia, come with us. We have to stick together, remember.' Fleur tried not to smile. The water felt good though and when she spied their three favourite young dolphins – Stormy, Jazz and Pearl – swimming steadily towards them she waved and called out a greeting.

'Can we swim out to meet them?' Mia pleaded.

'We're meant to be collecting wood,' Alfie pointed

out, glancing up the beach but seeing no sign of their mum and dad.

'Five minutes won't hurt,' Fleur decided, and she struck out with Mia towards Stormy, Jazz and Pearl.

The girls swam breaststroke, the water clear beneath them, until they reached the edge of a coral reef where the dolphins circled quietly. Then Jazz came up to Fleur and nuzzled her shoulder. His excited clicks meant that he was pleased to see her. 'You're a softie,' Fleur said with a grin as she wrapped both arms around Jazz's neck.

Meanwhile Mia squealed as fun-loving Stormy cleared the water, rolled in midair and landed with a splash. 'Come on, Alfie – what are you waiting for?' she yelled as he hesitated on the shoreline. 'Pearl wants to play with you!'

'OK, here I come.' Though Alfie still felt afraid of the water, the lure of the dolphins was too much – he plunged under to avoid the next breaker, kicked hard and resurfaced not far from Pearl, who greeted him with a mixture of gentle clicks and whistles. Testing the depth of the water, he found that his toes could only just touch the bottom and that there was a strong undertow, dragging him and the girls further out to sea. 'Watch out – we're drifting too far away from the shore,' he cried.

Fleur and Mia both felt the pull of the current and suddenly felt scared. Their hearts raced as they heaved themselves on to their dolphins' backs, where they could ride the swell of the waves in perfect safety. Alfie copied them and soon all three sat astride their dolphins and looked down into the blue depths at shoals of striped parrot fish darting beneath them, while forests of green, pink and brown seaweed swirled on the reef below. When they looked up again they were surprised to find that Jazz, Stormy and Pearl had carried them close to the rocks where *Merlin* had run aground.

The sight of the wreck made Alfie shudder. Her mast was gone, her propeller was mangled and her keel damaged beyond repair. She lay on her starboard side, her cockpit mostly underwater, her bow pointing upwards at a steep angle. As Pearl neared the wreck, she felt her passenger grow tense so she held back while

Jazz and Stormy carried Fleur and Mia closer still.

'Our poor boat,' Fleur sighed. Water lapped at *Merlin*'s damaged hull and she imagined the shoals of tiny, brightly coloured fishes swimming through the cabins into the saloon where the family had once eaten their meals.

Jazz circled the boat, taking Fleur within touching distance of the black rock that had pierced *Merlin*'s hull. Round and round she swam until Fleur finally figured out the reason why the dolphins had brought them here.

'I think Jazz is showing us we can go back on board,' she explained to Mia and Alfie. Her heart missed a beat as she imagined how hard this might be.

From his safe distance Alfie shook his head. 'Too dangerous,' he muttered.

'Maybe not.' Fleur began to study the capsized boat. *Merlin* was stuck fast between two pointed rocks and the only way she could shift would be if a high tide floated her free. 'We know the tide's going out. We'll be quite safe.'

'What for?' Mia wanted to know. She held tight to

Stormy's fin as he rode the rise and fall of the swelling waves. 'Why are we trying to get back on to *Merlin*?'

'To rescue things.' Fleur grew excited. This was too good a chance to miss. 'Not the electronic stuff – we know that's all ruined. But the first-aid kit, sharp knives, and ropes if we can find any – things we can use on the island.'

'How will we carry it back?' Alfie wanted to know. He didn't admit it, but the idea of climbing on to the boat made him feel sick with worry. What if, despite what Fleur said, their weight dislodged her from the rocks and she sank into the depths with them trapped inside?

'Maybe we'll find a rucksack in one of the cabins.' Fleur couldn't predict exactly how they would manage it but she knew they had to try. She stroked the side of Jazz's head then slowly slid from his back, hanging on to his flipper as she leaned out to take hold of the guardrail on the port side of the boat and only letting go when she was sure it wouldn't shift then slide free of the rocks. 'You two wait here,' she told Alfie and Mia.

They held their breaths and watched their brave

sister carefully haul herself on to the boat. She swung her legs over the rail then eased herself across the tilting deck towards the companionway.

'What's it look like?' Mia yelled as Fleur peered below deck.

Fleur stared down into the galley. 'Half of it is underwater. There are hundreds of little fishes swimming about but I think I can reach the drawer where we keep the knives. Let me find out.'

'Be careful!' Alfie's heart thumped against his ribs when he saw Fleur vanish.

Mia swallowed hard then began to count the seconds – *one, two, three* …

Down in the galley, Fleur ignored the neon-blue and sunshine-yellow fish. She picked her way between plastic plates and cups that floated on the surface. A wet tea towel hung from a rail and a carrier bag draped itself around her arm. When she opened the cupboard door, two plastic plates bobbed free.

Seven, eight, nine … Mia gulped again. Alfie's face was drained of colour. Stormy and Pearl held steady in one place while Jazz circled nearby.

With the sound of waves breaking on the rocks outside, Fleur held her breath, ducked underwater and wrenched open the drawer where they'd kept the cutlery. She groped around and grasped the nearest handle, came up for air and discovered that she'd found what she was looking for – the carving knife. Flushed with success, she ducked down a second time and came up with two more sharp knives.

Thirteen, fourteen, fifteen ... Mia and Alfie prayed for Fleur to reappear. They cheered with relief when she climbed up the companionway brandishing the plates and the knives. Jazz rose out of the water, head back, whistling his approval and flapping his flippers against his sides.

'There's lots more stuff!' Fleur promised. She disappeared again to collect more plates and cups which she stuffed into the carrier bag along with the knives. She emerged a second time, smiling and holding her trophies aloft.

'OK, time to get back!' Alfie didn't want Fleur to risk a third attempt. 'Jazz thinks so too,' he pointed out.

Fleur's dolphin swam close to the wreck and blew

out through the air hole on the top of his head. Then he gave a series of shrill whistles.

'I hear you.' Fleur saw the sense of carrying back what she'd already salvaged. With the bag in one hand she eased herself out of the galley and slithered on her belly across the deck. She ducked under the guardrail and slid into the water, grateful that Jazz was waiting for her to climb on his back.

'Now I could kick myself for not finding the first-aid kit,' she muttered as the dolphins turned for shore. 'That would have been way more useful than stupid plates and cups!'

'Never mind – it's too late now,' Alfie said.

'Are you glad we came for a swim?' Mia teased him. She felt the breeze on her face and arms and the splash of cold water on her legs as she turned to ask her question.

'Yes, but we'd better hold on tight,' he warned. 'Whoa!' Pearl went ahead with a surge of speed that tipped him backwards. With lightning-quick reactions he grabbed her fin and rode the waves alongside Mia and Stormy.

'So cool!' Fleur brought up the rear with Jazz. Through the spray raised by Pearl and Stormy's thrashing tail flukes she saw their beach with George's cave and the canopy of palm trees with a thin spiral of smoke rising from it. She smiled broadly, knowing that they had fire, food, fresh water and a whole island still to explore.

'What shall we call this island?' she asked Mia and Alfie as the dolphins slowed in the bay's shallow water to allow them to dismount. 'It's not on any of the maps and no one lives here so it's up to us to give it a name.'

'Shell Island,' Mia suggested, stooping to pick up a gleaming cream and pink conch shell that was rolling in the shallow waves.

Fleur said goodbye to Jazz then waded out of the water. 'George Island?' she wondered, thinking it would be nice to name the island after her gecko friend.

But Alfie stayed behind to stroke Pearl's beautiful domed head and run his hand down her velvety flank. He remembered the wild storm and the terrifying shipwreck and how they'd all been saved from drowning. 'No,' he argued, cupping his hand and gently lapping water over Pearl's sleek back. 'This has to be Dolphin Island.'

'Dolphin Island it is,' Mia and Fleur agreed and with broad smiles they sprinted up the beach, eager to tell their mum and dad.

Chapter Seven

'So we have been shipwrecked on Dolphin Island somewhere off the coast of Papua New Guinea.' James took stock after readily agreeing to the island's new name. He had stubble on his chin and his curly hair was caked with salt from the sea. Fleur could tell his cracked rib was aching more than ever. 'What else do we know about our new home?'

Fleur delved into her carrier bag, ready to bring out the first of her prized trophies – a plastic plate. 'We know it's miles from anywhere and it's about two miles long. It's got geckos and butterflies, gulls and parrots ...'

'Spiders, bats and bees,' Alfie interrupted.

'And fish,' Mia added.

'Coconuts.' Katie reminded them of the most obvious thing as she took the plates from Fleur. 'I'm not happy that you went off to search the wreck without asking,' she said with a shake of her head. 'Especially by yourselves.'

'We weren't by ourselves,' Mia protested. 'We were with Stormy.'

'And Jazz and Pearl,' Fleur added. After two days on Dolphin Island she was browner than ever and the auburn curls that hung low over her hazel eyes were turning light at the tips. 'Aren't you glad we've got plates?'

'Yes, they'll be useful.' Katie agreed.

'I still wish I'd rescued the first-aid stuff, though,' Fleur said with a sigh.

'Not to worry.' Katie studied the three excited faces, fresh from their latest adventure with the dolphins, and she softened. 'You did well,' she told them.

'And – ta-dah – I've got two small knives!' Fleur produced more items out of the bag.

'Excellent – I bet you've never been on a shopping trip like this before,' James said with a grin as he took them and set them down on the grass.

'And one big one!' Fleur had left the best until last.

The three blades glinted in the late afternoon sun as she held them up for all to see.

'That's excellent, Fleury.' James took the largest one. 'Think of all the things we can do with these!'

'Whittle sticks.' Alfie counted suggestions on his fingers. 'Cut down creepers, stab holes in coconuts to drink the milk ...'

'Gut and fillet fish.' James had been the chief cook on board *Merlin* and, despite his injury, he was determined to carry on in the job.

'Yuck!' Mia pulled a face.

'Yum!' Fleur and Alfie said as they rubbed their stomachs.

'I didn't have enough time to search the galley properly,' Fleur went on to explain. 'There are probably lots of other things that I couldn't carry. And more places to look.'

'We could certainly do with cutting down what's left of the sails and rigging and bringing them back here,' Katie decided. 'And rope would be useful, plus any chairs and sunloungers we can salvage.'

'*If* it's safe to go back!' James cautioned.

'That's what I said earlier,' Alfie grumbled quietly.

'Yes, he was Mr Sensible as usual.' Ignoring the moody expression on her brother's face, Fleur chattered on. 'I didn't even look in the cabins. Mine and Mia's and Alfie's are below sea level but yours is still clear of the water – I'm sure we can rescue lots of useful stuff from there – cushions, blankets, mattresses ...'

'But then how do we get them here?' Alfie bounced back with a logical question. 'They're too big to carry while we're riding the dolphins.'

'And anyway we can't rely on Pearl and company to be always at our beck and call,' Katie pointed out. 'They're wild creatures with a free run of the wide ocean. Who knows where they'll be tomorrow?'

The family discussion was taking place around the fire. The sun was low in the sky, casting a golden light on the eastern headland as it sank in the west. As they talked, Alfie used one of the small knives to whittle a sharp point on the calendar stick that he and Mia had begun that morning. He worked intently, listening hard and thinking as the others talked.

'I know – we could make a boat to row out to *Merlin* in!' Mia's face lit up with a broad grin.

'Easier said than done.' Katie patted Mia's arm and smiled. They sometimes forgot how young Mia was.

'So why don't we build a raft instead?' Fleur suggested. 'How hard can that be? All we need are logs tied together with creepers.'

'But would it stay afloat?' James wasn't sure that the waterlogged palm tree trunks that washed up on the beaches would be suitable. 'We'd need to build it out of dry wood and to be honest we need all we can gather to keep the fire going.'

For a while there was silence except for the crackle of burning wood and the flap of wings overhead as some of the parrots returned to roost. Beyond the dark headland to the west, a flock of white gulls soared soundlessly on wind currents, on the lookout for fish.

'Or we could keep the raft afloat with the big canisters,' Alfie suggested as if there hadn't been a gap. He stopped whittling then stood up to thrust the calendar stick deep in the ground.

'Which big canisters?' Fleur wanted to know.

Alfie looked out steadily from under his spiky fringe and gave his matter-of-fact answer. 'The ones I saw when we climbed the cliff to collect water.'

'Where?' Fleur, Mia, James and Katie said all at once.

'In the next cove but one,' Alfie replied. He pointed to the west. 'Four of them, about this big, stuck between some rocks. They've been there ages for all I know.'

∗

'I still say we should consider the risks before we do anything rash.' James was the one who kept everyone's feet on the ground. He pointed out that it was too late to set out on an expedition to fetch the canisters from the cove and that if Alfie was right about them being there for a long time, then they would still be in the same place tomorrow after they'd all had a good sleep.

Reluctantly Fleur, Alfie and Mia had to agree. Instead of scrambling over rocks to retrieve the canisters while their dad cooked the last of the fish and Katie went scouting for firewood, they used their new knives to cut and shape palm leaves into fans that they could use to swat flies.

'How will it work exactly?' Fleur asked Alfie, happy

that George had come to keep them company as the sun went down. The gecko had zigzagged swiftly across the beach from his cave towards their camp then slowed down and approached more cautiously when smoke from the fire wafted his way. Now he sat at a safe distance, taking an interest in the strange human activity that confronted him.

'How will what work?' Alfie answered Fleur's question with another question.

'The raft,' she explained. 'Why do we need the canisters?'

'It might *not* work,' he warned. 'Not if they don't have screw-tops. We need tops to keep the air in and the water out. That way they'll stay afloat. Then we'll make a platform out of light wood – not tree trunks 'cos – Dad's right – they're too heavy. What we really need is bamboo canes. They're nice and light.'

'Has anyone seen any bamboo growing on the island?' Fleur wondered.

Mia shot one hand in the air. 'Me – I have!' she exclaimed.

Everyone looked surprised.

'Do you even know what we're talking about?' Alfie challenged. Tears sprang into his little sister's hazel eyes and straight away he relented. After all, she was doing her best to help. 'OK, sorry, Mia – I believe you.'

'Show us in the morning,' Fleur murmured. She was still more interested in the canisters. 'So we tie the platform to the canisters and the whole thing floats like a lilo?'

Alfie nodded. 'Then one of us lies on our stomach and paddles with our arms.'

Fleur got the picture. 'Or else we find something that we can use as paddles and we make the platform big enough for two people. That would be better.'

'And we only go out on it when the sea is calm.' As usual Alfie wanted to stay away from big waves and strong undercurrents. 'Half a mile is a long way – we'll have to wait for the right conditions.'

'But think of what else we'll be able to salvage,' Fleur sighed, gazing out to sea at the wreck. 'Maybe I can bring another T-shirt and some clean shorts back to the island – even sunglasses and flip-flops if they're still floating around.'

'Will Monkey be there?' Mia wondered about her favourite soft toy. He'd come everywhere with her since she'd been a toddler and though his brown fur was worn and he only had one eye, he was still the thing she missed the most.

'I don't know but we can find out,' Alfie promised. He didn't tell anybody but he was most looking forward to finding the boat's mechanical compass. He would bring it back, take it apart, dry it out then put it back together in full working order.

Their mum interrupted their daydreams by preparing to throw another heavy piece of driftwood on to the fire. 'Stand well back,' she warned.

The branch landed and threw up a fountain of bright sparks which sent George scurrying off and roused the parrots from their roosts. Four vivid shapes squawked and screeched, flapped their wings and rose into the twilit sky. Two bright red feathers twirled to earth. Mia jumped up and caught them. She crawled into the shelter and found her sunhat then stuck the quills into the band so that they stood up straight like feathers in a native islander's headdress. Then she danced back out into the open, skipping and spinning on the spot to show off her new creation.

The scarlet feathers glowed in the flickering firelight. Fleur laughed and clapped at Mia's crazy dance. Alfie cooled his flushed face with his new fan.

'Supper's ready!' James called, serving barbequed fish on to plates and setting them out in a circle around the fire. 'Mia, Alfie, Fleur – stop what you're doing. It's time to eat!'

Chapter Eight

That night Fleur found it hard to sleep. It was her mum's casual remark about Jazz, Pearl and Stormy being wild dolphins that bothered her and kept her awake.

It was true, there was a big ocean out there – hundreds if not thousands of miles of empty blue sea for the small pod to range over in their daily hunt for fish and squid. Fleur pictured Pearl, Jazz and Stormy diving deep amongst shoals of angelfish and groupers, stingrays and sea turtles, staying under for minutes at a time before rising for air. They would feed then take time out to play – leaping and diving, spinning and flipping through the air.

They'll swim far away and forget all about us, Fleur thought sadly as she stared up at the silver moon and stars. Waves broke and crashed on to the shore. At daybreak, while the others slept, she crept from the shelter and walked down to the sea.

'Please don't go,' she murmured, scanning the empty horizon in the half-light. She felt the breeze on her face and soft, cool sand between her toes. No dolphins swam to meet her.

Waves lapped her ankles. A sliver of golden sun crept into view and spread its molten light over the ocean. The grey sky turned pink. 'We need you,' Fleur whispered, watching and waiting with a heavy heart.

*

Back in the shelter, Mia woke to the sight of a furry centipede crawling across her yellow life vest, a few centimetres from her face. Her eyes flashed wide open and she froze. 'Alfie – help!' she whimpered.

'What's wrong?' Already awake and wondering where Fleur had got to, Alfie sat up to see the centipede on Mia's makeshift pillow. 'Don't move,' he muttered. 'Those centipedes bite. Stay there while I find a stick.'

'What will you do – squish it?' Mia asked with a shiver. The creature had a brown and red body and lots of tiny legs. She didn't like the look of it at all.

'No.' Alfie placed his stick in front of the centipede and waited for it to climb on board. 'I'm going to save him and put him in the bushes.'

His plan was a success and seconds later Alfie carried the centipede outside.

By now Katie and James were rubbing their eyes and stretching and Fleur had returned from her dawn vigil by the sea. Quickly recovering from the centipede scare, Mia jumped up to mark their third day on the calendar stick before she put on her headdress and cape and dashed outside to search for more feathers.

'I'm slow to get into gear this morning,' the children's dad admitted as he sat up. 'I ache all over. Rib, legs, arms – everything.'

'Poor old man,' Katie teased, then grew serious. 'You don't feel feverish, do you?'

'No. Maybe a bit dehydrated though. We all have to remember to drink plenty in this heat.'

'I'm on water duty,' Fleur volunteered with a cheery smile. She liked the idea of climbing up to the spring and getting a good view of the sea. Surely from up there she would be certain to spot the dolphins.

'You're OK to take Mia?' Katie handed Fleur the empty bottles and watched her put them inside the carrier bag. 'If you two fetch water, your dad and I can look for those canisters with Alfie. Let's all aim to be back here for mid-morning – we'll have to judge the time by the height of the sun.'

'OK – no problem.' Fleur was eager to start but before she and Mia set off they all agreed that whoever was back first should collect more wood.

'The fire is our top priority,' James reminded everyone. His aches and pains seemed to make him grumpy. 'It comes before larking around with dolphins or making fancy headdresses.'

'Come on, Mia – let's show him we mean business.' Fleur led the way to the foot of the cliff and chose the easiest route up. Tying the carrier bag to the strap of her swimsuit, she began the climb.

Meanwhile Alfie, Katie and James set off for the western headland. They picked their way over the rocks into the small cove where Katie and James had first come ashore. From there they would have to scramble over another outcrop of rocks into a wider bay where Alfie had spotted the canisters.

Halfway up the cliff on their separate mission, Fleur and Mia paused for breath. They looked down on to their beach at three small figures making their way across the sand, their shadows long and thin in the low morning sun. 'Let's hope Alfie's right about the

canisters,' Fleur said. 'It's a long way for Dad to walk if he's wrong.'

Mia nodded then forged ahead, dislodging small stones as she climbed. 'Is it OK if I paddle in the stream?' she asked.

'Yes, if you're careful.' Fleur dodged the stones and followed her.

Mia hurried on until she came to the bubbling spring. Straight away she plunged her feet into the cool, fresh stream.

'I bet that feels nice.' Fleur arrived soon after and did the same. 'Ooh, yes – it's so good,' she sighed. She gazed up at the thick forest on the steep hill that rose behind the cliff and found herself wondering what kind of animals might lurk in its shadows. There would be bats for sure and loads more butterflies and birds, plus little things like iguanas, skinks, snakes and geckos. She didn't think there would be big animals like wild boars because how would they have got on to the island in the first place? On the other hand …

Fleur turned her back on the forest and raised her hand to shield her eyes from the sun's glare. She looked out to sea. *Merlin* was still there, of course – her bow pointing up towards the sky, her hull letting in water, her cabins alive with bright blue and yellow angelfish. Behind the wrecked boat the sea sparkled and stretched on for ever.

'Where are our dolphins?' Mia wanted to know.

'They must be busy,' Fleur said with a sigh, then did her best to hide her disappointment. Untying the carrier bag, she took out the bottles and gave one to Mia. 'Let's fill these up then get back as fast as we can.'

Fleur and Mia sank the bottles under the surface and listened to the gurgling sound of water pouring in. They lifted them out and screwed on the tops and were about to put them back in the bag when Mia had an idea.

'Why don't we fill the bag as well?' she suggested.

'We could try,' Fleur agreed. Carefully she lowered the bag into the water then held it up to check for leaks. Luckily there were no holes. 'Good thinking,' she told Mia as she tied a tight knot in the top of the bulging bag.

After one last dangle of their feet in the refreshing stream, they made their way across the steep slope and down the cliff. They were back to base with the day's water supply long before the others returned with the canisters.

By now the sun was scorching so Fleur and Mia put on their hats and went out to scavenge for driftwood, first fetching more from George's cave then wandering off in the opposite direction to see what else had been washed up since they last searched the beach.

'Will this burn?' Mia pointed to a heap of dried seaweed stuck between some rocks. She poked at it with a stick then quickly jumped away. 'Dead jellyfish!' she cried.

'Don't touch it.' Fleur shuddered. She loved animals but even she couldn't stand the sight of a slimy jellyfish splatted on a rock. 'We've collected enough wood to keep us going for a bit. Let's go back and have a coconut snack.'

In any case she'd noticed dark clouds gathering rapidly in the east and felt a stiff breeze start to blow. If rain was coming it would be best for her and Mia to take shelter.

So they hurried back and stoked up the fire then sat anxiously watching and waiting. Within minutes the clouds had covered the sun and the whole sky turned grey. Out to sea, wind whipped the waves into dark green, mountainous peaks that rolled in and crashed on to the shore.

'Here it comes,' Fleur grumbled as she huddled with Mia under their thatched roof. 'Mum, Dad and Alfie had better hurry up, or they'll get soaked.'

Too late – large raindrops spattered down on to the sand, slowly at first then faster and harder. They bounced off the boulders and pounded the broad leaves of the bushes behind the Fishers' shelter. Needles of rain pierced the tree canopy and lashed down on to the burning logs, making them sizzle, hiss and smoke.

Then the lightning started, forking through the black sky with a blinding flash followed by a crack of thunder. Each crack made Fleur and Mia tremble and retreat further from the entrance, hugging each other in the dark shadows and praying for the storm to end.

Still the rain came down and the waves crashed, lightning split the sky and thunder crashed.

'What about the others?' Mia whimpered. 'Will they be all right?'

'They'll be fine,' Fleur told her. 'They'll find somewhere to shelter.'

Then large wet drops began to trickle through the gaps in their palm leaf roof and plop heavily to the floor – slowly at first, then faster, so that Fleur had to hold Mia's cloak over their heads to keep them dry. She watched anxiously and waited for the storm to end.

Finally the thunder and lightning ceased and the rain turned to warm drizzle. Fleur crept to the doorway and peered out into the gloom. For a few moments she wondered why it was so dark. Flames from the fire should still be giving them some light in spite of the storm clouds. Oh no – the fire!

Fleur's stomach tied itself into a knot. 'The fire's gone out!' she gasped.

Mia came to join her.

They stared at a pile of grey ashes and wet, black logs. There was no smoke, no spark of life.

'What do we do now?' Mia whimpered.

Fleur's face was blank. She shivered from head to foot. Fire meant everything here on Dolphin Island. It was more important than anything else – fire for cooking, fire for keeping warm at night, fire as a signal for any passing plane or ship. Now it was dead – the storm had killed it and she was the one who had let it happen. Mia began to cry and the others were missing.

Still the dolphins were nowhere to be seen.

*

West of the camp, Alfie felt good as he led the expedition to locate the canisters. He knew exactly where to find them and even though the scramble over the second headland took longer than expected because of his dad's injury, he still hoped they'd be back to base by mid-morning as planned.

'Slow down!' James called as Alfie and Katie forged ahead. The pain in his ribs had got worse and he couldn't help lagging behind. 'I'm definitely not in good shape,' he admitted.

'I can see the canisters – they're exactly where I said!' Alfie pointed to a big jumble of seaweed and storm debris trapped between smooth boulders at the far side of the new cove. In amongst the rubbish were the four large plastic containers he'd seen from the high vantage point above the cliff.

'Brilliant. We'll have to call you Eagle Eye Alfie from now on.' Katie put an arm around his shoulder and gave him a quick hug. 'You go on ahead. I'll wait for your dad.'

So Alfie jumped down from the rocks and ran on, leaving a curved trail of footprints on the untouched sand and only slowing down when he approached a swarm of black flies buzzing around the rubbish. He needed something to swat them away but there were no handy palm fronds lying on the beach so instead he stooped to pick up a large pebble and throw it at the heap. The flies rose into the humid air, buzzing angrily.

'Scoot!' Alfie yelled, swiping at them with his skinny arms. 'Get away!'

It was no good – the flies came straight back, so Alfie took a deep breath then clamped his hand over his nose and mouth. Flies or no flies, he was going in!

'Good job, Alfie!' His mum's voice reached him as he kicked at the first container to dislodge it from the pile. She was alone and it took Alfie a while to spot his dad still stuck on the rocky headland. 'I told Dad to stay there and rest,' she explained when she drew near. 'Perhaps he shouldn't have come, but I guess he was putting on a brave face for us.'

With his hand still covering his mouth, Alfie freed a second canister then stood back from the heap to draw breath. So far, so good – the four-litre containers still had their tops, though they were dented and their labels showing pictures of large yellow sunflowers were scuffed and torn.

'It looks as if they were used for storing cooking oil,' Katie guessed. 'You know what crews on some of these big container ships are like – they chuck empty stuff overboard even if it's not biodegradable.'

'Lucky for us.'

'As it turns out,' Katie agreed before taking a deep breath and delving into the mess to retrieve two more containers.

She and Alfie lined up all four in the sand and studied them. 'What do you think?' he asked.

'They'll come in very handy. Whether they'll make good buoyancy aids for our raft, I'm not so sure.'

'But we can try.' Alfie picked up two bulky containers, tucked one under each arm and set off back towards the rocks. 'Uh-oh,' he muttered when he spotted clouds on the horizon.

His mum nodded. 'Rain is on its way. We have to expect it on a tropical island, I guess.'

The wind got up as they hurried on, blustering and whipping up sand into their faces so they scrunched their eyes and peered through half-closed lids. They reached James as the first cold raindrops started to fall.

'How are you feeling now?' For once Katie couldn't disguise her concern.

'I'll live,' James replied, standing up with a grimace. He looked at the darkening sky. 'I'll have to take my time getting back so why don't you two go on ahead.'

'And leave you to the mercy of the storm?' Alfie's mum was having none of it. 'All for one ...'

'And one for all!' Alfie declared. He ducked his head to keep the rain off his face and led the way down from the rocky outcrop.

'You heard the boy!' Now Katie was the one who put on a brave smile. She heard thunder in the distance and expected lightning any time. Meanwhile, raindrops lashed their bare skin. 'Let's keep walking, one foot after another, steady as we go.'

Chapter Nine

The storm raged and Alfie, Katie and James made slow progress over the rocks into the narrow inlet. They fought against wind and rain, but when lightning struck far out to sea and thunder deafened them they made a hasty decision to take shelter under a rocky overhang.

'Uh-oh, it looks like we're not the only ones.' Alfie reached the rock and was about to place his containers on to the ground when a large black insect scuttled between his feet. 'Watch out – scorpion!' He recognized its shiny body armour and long, curved tail with its bulbous sack of poison at the tip.

The scorpion was gone almost as soon as Alfie spotted it – squeezing itself into a rock crevice out of sight. Nonetheless Katie and James trod cautiously under the overhang.

'Let's hope this rain doesn't last much longer.' James scanned the dramatic build-up of ragged, dark clouds. By now the wind had whipped the sea into a frenzy of crashing waves which covered the rocks in a heavy white spray. But it was the electrical storm that made them most afraid – blinding flashes of lightning that forked across the watery horizon and died, immediately followed by ear-splitting claps of thunder. Light and then darkness. An angry roar then silence, with the whole island straining against the wild force of the wind.

'Yes and let's hope Fleur and Mia are OK,' Katie muttered as thunder crashed again and again and rain came down more heavily than ever.

Alfie kept firm hold of his two containers as he crouched under the overhang. There was nothing out there but waves and spray, wind and mist. *Maybe this is why the dolphins left the island,* he thought. *I don't know how they did it, but they worked out that a storm was on its way.*

*

Back at base, Fleur and Mia sank to the ground beside

the ashes of their dead fire. Cold drops splashed down from the tree canopy on to their bare heads and made them shiver. They mingled with the tears that were already trickling down their cheeks.

'Don't bother – it won't do any good,' Fleur told Mia when she leaned forward to poke the ashes back to life.

Mia wiped her wet face with sooty hands, leaving black streaks down her cheeks. 'Will we get into trouble?'

Fleur shook her head. 'Not you. It wasn't your fault – it was mine. I'm thirteen. You're only six. It was my job to keep the fire going.'

Mia stood up to examine a stack of firewood propped against a rock. 'It's sopping wet,' she said miserably.

Fleur looked up at the sky to see that the storm clouds were already clearing and the sun had begun to shine through. From its position in the sky she could tell that it must be nearly midday – much later than the time that their mum had said they'd be back. She lowered her gaze to watch storm petrels – fluttering, bat-like birds – dive into the shallow waves and catch what looked from this distance like small crabs.

Further out, two pelicans flapped lazily across the wide bay. Then to her amazement, there – just clear of the horizon – she made out a small object moving across a patch of blue sky.

'Plane!' Fleur jumped up. Her heart was in her mouth as she ran down the beach to the water's edge. A white plane was heading towards Dolphin Island – the first they'd seen since they'd been shipwrecked.

Mia followed her, slowed down by the soft, wet sand. 'Where?' she cried.

Fleur pointed. 'There – climbing higher, coming closer!'

'Hey!' Mia spotted it then raised her arms above her head and waved.

'We don't have a fire – they won't see our signal,' Fleur realized. Her stomach fluttered with terrible panic. The plane grew larger – she could make out the jet engines on the wings but it was still too far away and too high in the sky to hear them.

Mia waved and yelled while Fleur ran back to the shelter for the piece of white sailcloth. She sprinted back to the shore and began to wave it like a flag to attract the pilot's attention.

The plane kept on coming and now there was a faint drone from its engines.

'Look at us – we're down here!' Mia cried. Why wasn't it flying lower and taking a proper look at the beach? Why was the pilot ignoring them?

'Take this.' Fleur passed her the cloth. She looked around in the jetsam thrown up by the storm and seized a waterlogged stick. Using one end, she began to write huge letters in the sand. H – E – L – P!

The noise of the engines grew louder but the plane was still so high in the sky that Fleur and Mia could only just make out the shape of the cockpit and the row of small windows in the plane's side. Then, without warning, just before it reached Dolphin Island, the pilot at the controls made it bank steeply to the west, away from Fleur's hastily written message.

'Where are you going? Come back!' Mia wailed.

Fleur took back the cloth and waved frantically.

Still the plane veered away from the island and chose a new course over open water. As it left, there was a flash of sunlight reflected in the cockpit windows and the dying drone of its engines.

Fleur and Mia's hopes sank as they watched it grow smaller. Their shoulders sagged and Fleur let the cloth trail in the water. A wave curled on to the beach. It reached her message and washed away the letters one by one. With it went all chance of rescue.

*

The minute the lightning stopped Alfie, Kate and James came out from under the rocky overhang, took up the cooking oil canisters and continued on their homeward trek. It had been a bad storm but, like the typhoon that had wrecked *Merlin*, it was soon over.

'Look at the mess it's dumped on the beach,' Katie grumbled as they made their way through uprooted sea grass, glass bottles, broken shells and sharp, brittle pieces of dead coral which were hard on the feet and had to be avoided.

'Never mind that – do you see what I see?' James dropped his canisters and made Alfie and Katie look up at a small passenger plane heading their way.

Katie shielded her eyes. 'Oh my goodness! From this distance it looks like a small private jet – probably flying off its original course to steer clear of the storm.'

'Too far away for us to be seen,' James warned Alfie in case he got his hopes up. 'There's no chance from that height, I'm afraid.'

'But the pilot might see our fire.' Alfie doggedly refused to believe that the plane could pass over Dolphin Island without seeing them. He raced ahead and started to scramble up the headland, desperate to see the plume of smoke rising out of the tree canopy in the next bay.

The white wings tilted as the plane altered course through wispy clouds. Alfie reached the crest of the rocky outcrop and looked for the fire that would attract the pilot's attention and bring him back to investigate. He could see the palm trees below the cliff and knew exactly where the smoke should rise but no matter how much he screwed up his eyes, he couldn't make it out.

What's happened to the fire? Where are Mia and Fleur? Alarm shot through Alfie and, without waiting for Katie and James to catch up, he hurried on. Overhead, the small jet plane continued to swing away from the island and climb higher in the sky. Alfie reached their beach and sprinted breathlessly past George's cave towards their shelter, only coming to a halt when he saw the black remains of the fire that might have saved them.

From inside the sodden shelter, a distraught Mia saw a pair of skinny, sand-covered legs, the bottom of some red swimming shorts and two white plastic containers. 'Oh, Alfie – the fire went out!' she sobbed. 'The plane didn't see Fleur's writing in the sand. And now no one will ever know we're here on Dolphin Island – not ever!'

Chapter Ten

Alfie set his containers down at the entrance to the shelter then stared at the mess of wet ashes and partly burned wood. He bit his lip to fight back tears then shrugged. 'Never mind, Mia – don't cry. We can start all over again.'

Straight away he started to pull the remains of the fire apart, setting to one side any wood that could be dried out then re-used. 'We saw the plane too. It probably wouldn't have noticed us anyway, even if we'd had the fire. It was too high up and it changed course before it got here.'

Fleur took a deep breath, pushed her hair behind her ears and sighed. Then she took up a branch and used it as a broom to sweep the soggy ashes under a shrub. 'What's happened to Mum and Dad? How come they're lagging so far behind?'

'Dad's ribs still hurt,' Alfie explained. 'I reckon he'll need to rest up for a bit.'

Sure enough, when James and Katie eventually arrived, Katie led their dad straight into the shelter and arranged life vests as a cushion for him to lean against. 'It looks to me like you've started a fever, so you're not going anywhere until you feel better,' she told him. 'I'm taking over as cook while you take things easy for a few days.'

Fleur overheard the new plan. 'Nobody will be cooking anything unless we get another fire going,' she muttered to Mia and Alfie.

'Or catch some more fish,' Alfie agreed. 'But, like I said, we have to begin again – fire first then fish.'

'What do you think, George?' Fleur was pleased to glance up and see her gecko hanging upside down at the entrance to the shelter. 'Can we catch fish by ourselves, without the dolphins?'

With a quick flick of his tail, George flipped himself up on to the roof and found a good position from where he could watch the action – Alfie sorting wood, Fleur sweeping, Mia searching for dry straw under the broad-leaved shrubs.

'Can we do it?' they chorused. 'Yes, we can!' It was wonderful how their mood lifted the minute the sun shone again and steam started to rise from the forest trees on the hills above, for what was the point of dwelling on bad luck and missed opportunity?

'Just look at how much we've done already and it's only Day 3,' Fleur reminded everyone. She and Mia began to arrange a heap of straw topped by small pyramid of twigs. 'We've made a shelter ...'

'That happens to let in water!' Alfie grinned as he laid out wood to dry in the sun.

'Whatever!' Fleur shrugged this off. 'We've learned to catch fish ...'

'Only because Pearl and the others showed us how,' he reminded her.

'We've gone out to the wreck and brought back knives, cups and plates.'

'Ditto!'

'And soon we'll build a raft and go out there again.' Her job done, Mia started to dig a deep hole in the sand with her hands, just for fun. A curious George soon came to join her, bringing a friend with him. The two geckos perched at the edge of the hole, peering down. Meanwhile, Katie emerged from the shelter and suggested to Fleur and Alfie that they left the wood to dry for a while before they started rubbing sticks together to make a spark. 'Your dad's taking a nap,' she informed them. 'Why don't you make yourselves scarce? Go down to the sea and work out how to catch our supper.'

'Cool!' Alfie spoke for all three of them. 'Mia, where's your cloak?'

By this time, Mia's hole in the sand was waist-deep and George and his mate had snuck off across the sand, back to the bat cave for their own little siesta. 'It's in the shelter,' she told Alfie, who crept inside to fetch their improvised fishing net without waking James.

Then the kids set off under the hot sun, complete with sunhats, using the tattered sailcloth as a wide parasol and stepping carefully through debris from the recent rainstorm.

'Bagsy I have this!' Mia cried, stooping to pick up a

length of blue nylon rope and tying it around her waist.

'Hey – a conch shell!' Alfie declared. He raised it to his lips and experimented with blowing into the narrow end to make a trumpet sound. He puffed out his cheeks then blew, but there was only a faint whine and then a splutter. Alfie threw it down on the sand in disgust.

'Come on – we'll never catch any fish at this rate.' Fleur stepped out from under the makeshift parasol and into the waves that rippled along the shoreline. She scanned the familiar headlands to east and west. 'Maybe we'll find little tiddlers in rock pools – ones that got left behind when the tide went out.'

'Or crabs,' Alfie suggested. 'We've seen petrels catch crabs so there must be some around.'

With the hot sun on their backs, they headed to the eastern rocks, where they found the pools they were looking for but no crabs.

Fleur frowned and stared into the first empty pool. The water was crystal-clear but all she could see were three spiky black sea urchins and one little starfish.

Alfie crouched down to lift a loose rock. 'Nothing,' he reported as he peered underneath.

'Ooh!' For a moment, Mia's breathless cry raised their hopes. She was pointing to the next beach – one that they hadn't yet explored.

Alfie and Fleur looked hard and finally realized what Mia had spotted.

A creature about a metre long had emerged from the sea and was waddling laboriously over the white sand, pushing slowly forward on splayed flippers. Its flat head poked out from a large, domed shell.

'Sea turtle.' Alfie was impressed. He forgot all about fishing and ran to take a closer look.

'Here comes another.' Mia was close on Alfie's heels. She pointed to a second turtle making its clumsy way out of the water.

'I don't think we should get too close,' Fleur warned from a distance of twenty paces. She thought the turtles were amazing – patiently plodding out of the sea with their scaly yellow heads, beady eyes and beautifully patterned shells, seemingly ignoring the intruders on their beach.

'They look like dinosaurs.' For once, Mia managed to stay still and to keep her voice low.

Fleur wondered why they were here. 'Maybe they're coming ashore to lay their eggs, except no – it's not the right time of year.'

'Or just to sunbathe,' Mia suggested.

'Or maybe the storm altered the rip currents and confused them.' Alfie's rumbling stomach reminded him that he'd read somewhere about being able to make turtle soup. 'You know, people eat them,' he said in a low, uneasy voice.

'No way!' Fleur and Mia shot back.

Their raised voices must have startled the turtles because they both stopped and turned their heads. Spotting the intruders, they shuffled around and with a sudden, surprising burst of speed they hurried back the way they'd come.

'I was only saying ...' Alfie protested. 'I didn't mean ...'

'Good, I'm glad.' Fleur was happy to see the turtles wade back into the water. Within seconds they were surrounded by shallow breakers that washed over their shells and lifted them off the ground. Using their front flippers like paddles, they swam out to sea then down under the waves and out of sight.

'Honestly, I didn't mean …' Alfie was upset that Fleur thought he could really have eaten turtle soup.

'It's OK.' She sighed as she turned her face to the sun and led the way back to the headland. 'We're all hungry – I know that. But fish is what we came for and at this rate it'll be dark before we catch any.'

As they reached the rocks, Alfie stopped to gaze up at the cliffs rising from the beach. He recognized the shape of the hillside and landmarks like the white waterfall splashing over dark rocks below the spring and the conical peak of rock rising from the dark green forest. 'It's weird how Dolphin Island feels like our home now.'

Fleur glanced back at her brother, his body brown as a hazelnut, his cheeks flecked by white salt where the sea spray had dried, the brim of his hat blown back by the breeze. Somehow he looked sad. 'It is home,' she said quietly.

For a while their thoughts drifted back to their old home, to their pretty house by the tree-lined river, next door to Gran and Granddad.

Mia slipped her hand into Alfie's. 'Would you like

me to make you a shell necklace after I've finished one for Fleur?' she asked.

Alfie nodded and squeezed her hand. 'First we have to catch some fish,' he said in a firm voice, scrambling up on to the rocks ahead of them both.

*

'No luck?' Katie asked after Fleur, Alfie and Mia had spent the afternoon trying to catch supper. She joined them on the headland and sat on a rock looking thoughtfully out to sea.

'Not yet.' They'd been there for what seemed like hours but Alfie wasn't ready to give in. 'We've seen plenty of fish swimming past – big things like groupers and snappers – but they're all too far out for us to catch.'

'And we don't have any bait,' Fleur said with a frown.

Katie had left James sleeping and was racking her brains over what to do next. 'Alfie – we're running low on coconuts. How about we collect some more?'

Recognizing the determined look on his mum's face, Alfie left the sailcloth with Fleur and Mia and set off up the beach with her.

This left the girls alone on the headland with their

empty stomachs growling and with fading hopes of catching anything in their 'net'.

'The fish are laughing at us.' Mia made a sad face as she peered into the water at a decent-sized grouper lazily swimming by. The grouper seemed to peer up at her and grin.

'Uh-oh, they'd better watch out – they won't be laughing soon!' Fleur had glanced up and caught a first glimpse of what she'd spent all day desperately longing to see. At last – there was movement on the horizon, creatures leaping and whistling, surging through the waves and speeding towards their bay. Recent fears melted away as she saw a dozen dolphins coming to their aid.

The second Mia saw the dolphins, she jumped up and shouted, 'Hurray, you came back just in time!'

The dolphins drew nearer, playing as they swam. Fleur picked Jazz out from the rest as he leaped in the air higher and longer than any of the others then landed and rose up again out of the water to do a spectacular tail-walk across the bay. Stormy too was easy to spot at the head of the pod, his dark fin cutting through the water at top speed. *But where was little Pearl?* Fleur and Mia wondered.

They needn't have worried. As the pod swam near, a small, smooth head popped up only a few metres from their dangling feet. Pearl gave a shrill squeak followed by some chattering clicks. Then she blew air from her blowhole, waiting for another dolphin to surface beside her. The big newcomer eyed Fleur and Mia warily then nudged Pearl with her blunt snout until Pearl came alongside under the shelter of the older dolphin's flipper.

'I'm guessing that's Pearl's mother,' Fleur whispered. 'She's got the same pink belly and big, bright eyes.'

'And smiley mouth,' Mia added.

Fleur noticed how the mother dolphin kept Pearl close to her side until she'd finished checking them out. 'That's so sweet!'

'It's OK – we're Pearl's friends,' Mia explained, fearlessly slipping from her rock into the water and swimming out to the mother and daughter.

With a playful squeak, Pearl broke away and came to meet Mia, who took a gulp of air then kicked her legs and disappeared underwater, inviting Pearl to come and explore the small coral reef close to the rocks.

'Don't worry – Mia can swim like a fish,' Fleur told the mother dolphin. 'They'll be back soon.' While they waited for the pair to return she thought up a name for the mother then said it out loud. 'Marina,' she decided. 'Pearl and Marina – that sounds cool.'

Under the surface Mia and Pearl swam with darting, brightly coloured fish until they came face to face with a curious stingray. Its gliding, ghostly appearance quickly sent Mia on her way, followed soon after by Pearl. The two of them reappeared on the surface in a rush of bubbles.

Satisfied that Pearl was in good company, Marina circled the happy pair then with a flick of her tail flukes she plunged out of sight.

It was time to get serious, Fleur decided. She stepped from the rocks and showed Pearl the square piece of sailcloth. 'We need more fish!'

Straight away Pearl seemed to understand. She left off playing and swam to fetch the rest of the pod while Mia waded out of the water and joined Fleur. The girls waited for a few minutes, keeping a close eye on activity at sea. They saw dorsal fins cutting swiftly across the bay as the dolphins approached. This time they swam towards shore in a V-shaped formation and it was soon possible to see shoals of fish being herded into the shallows, in between the rocks where Fleur and Mia stood.

'They're so wonderful and clever,' Fleur said softly. It was amazing how Pearl had realized what she wanted them to do and how quickly she'd organized the rest of the pod.

Hundreds of silver fish soon twisted and turned between the girls' legs or flopped out of the water in a panic as, with a swift pincer movement, the dolphin army closed in. Mia caught one leaping silver fish between her hands and held on to it as she and Fleur lowered the cloth and dredged it through the water, coming up with four more.

'Thank you!' Fleur held up the bulging, dripping cloth for Jazz to see. He broke away from the formation and swam up to nuzzle her legs. She bent and stroked his back then planted a kiss on the top of his head.

'Thank you, Stormy! Thank you, Pearl!' Mia grinned. 'We've got five fish – that's one each for supper.'

Their job done, the pod bobbed lazily in the silvery shallows and splashed their tails. *Only too happy to help friends in need*, they seemed to say as Fleur and Mia turned with the day's catch and headed for home.

Chapter Eleven

Next day Alfie woke to the screeching of gulls and the crash of waves on the shore. Mia was already awake, humming to herself as she made a fourth charcoal mark on the calendar stick. Though Katie and James were still fast asleep, Fleur was nowhere to be seen.

Easing his stiff limbs, Alfie rubbed his eyes then quietly joined Mia at the entrance to the shelter. 'Where's Fleur?' he whispered.

'She went exploring,' Mia told him casually.

Alfie frowned then scanned the empty beach and shoreline. 'Exploring where?'

'She didn't say.' Mia finished marking the calendar then went out to scout for more parrot feathers.

As Alfie followed her, he looked up and caught sight of Fleur picking her way up the cliff in her pink swimsuit and white T-shirt. She paused to glance down and when she saw him she held up the water bottles and waved.

'Fleur's not exploring, she's gone for water.' Still grumpy about being woken, Alfie refused to be excited about Mia's latest find – a curved yellow feather from a cockatoo's crest. Day 4 on Dolphin Island hadn't got off to a good start as far as he was concerned – first the raucous gulls and now he noticed that his insect bites had crept up his legs on to his stomach and they itched like crazy. On top of that, Fleur had beaten him to his favourite job of bringing back drinking water.

'You know last night – Mum and Dad said we could build the raft today,' Mia reminded him with a sunny smile. She inspected the row of four big containers lined up in the sand. 'Shall we do it before they wake up, as a surprise?'

'No way. It'll take us the whole day, silly.' Alfie tried to squish her enthusiasm as if he was stamping on one of the pesky, blood-sucking sandflies. 'First we have to find the stuff to build it with – long, straight branches, or bamboo canes – if we can find any. Then we have to cut them down and carry them back. That's before we even start.'

'I know where the bamboo is – really, I do!' With enthusiasm unsquished, Mia stuck the yellow feather in her hat beside the two red ones then strode out across the beach towards the eastern headland – a small figure in a turquoise swimming costume, brown hair tucked up under her home-made hat. 'Come on, slowcoach!' she called back to Alfie.

He followed grumpily, stopping to pick up a sharp knife from the wire grate by the steadily burning fire, then dragging his feet through the soft sand. *No way does Mia know what she's talking about,* he thought. *This is a wild-goose chase.*

On she went, up and over the rocks in a flash and down into the unexplored cove where they'd seen the sea turtles. The sun was still low in the east, casting a soft light that tinged the wings of the soaring gulls with pink.

Mia marched on ahead, up the beach, between coconut palms into a narrow, sheltered clearing where long grass grew and leaves rustled in the breeze.

'See!' she said, pointing to a group of tall, swaying canes topped by slender, spear-shaped leaves.

'Whoa!' The discovery jerked Alfie out of his bad mood and he surveyed the unexpected crop of bamboo with a delighted grin. 'Good job, Mia.'

'See,' she repeated stubbornly, standing with legs wide apart and frowning at him from under the brim of her multicoloured hat.

'OK, you were right. I'm sorry.' Taking the knife from the waistband of his shorts, Alfie ventured with Mia in amongst the rustling bamboo canes. At over two metres tall, they towered over them, but each cane was slender – perhaps three centimetres at the base, tapering off towards the top. 'We're going to need a lot of these to make a big enough platform,' Alfie warned Mia. 'And it won't be easy to carry them back over the rocks. We might have to make more than one journey.'

'What are we waiting for?' she said eagerly.

So he set to, using the sharp blade to hack through the base of the canes and handing each one to Mia, who stripped the leaves from them then laid them carefully on the grass until they had a stack of about thirty.

'That's enough for now,' Alfie decided. Cutting down bamboo canes was sweaty, thirsty work. Besides, their mum and dad would be awake and wondering where they'd got to. 'We'll take these home and come back later for some more.'

Alfie took up one end of the canes and waited for Mia to lift the other. Together they set off across the beach.

*

It took Fleur longer than usual to reach the spring because she stopped to inspect each butterfly, bird and flower on the way. How could a butterfly's wing be so delicate and bright – the blue so deep and metallic, the orange so sizzling hot? And cockatoos, when she got close to them, were bigger than she expected. One perched on an overhanging branch watching with beady eyes as she filled her water bottles. He puffed out his white chest feathers and unfurled his yellow crest then opened his curved beak and let out an angry squawk.

'It's OK – I'm done here,' Fleur said with a smile and a nervous glance up at the forested hillside. A sudden thought had crossed her mind – perhaps she could find something in the forest that would help when it came to building the raft? 'I plan to leave the bottles between these rocks and climb up a little way. I'll collect them on my way down.'

The cockatoo bobbed his head up and down, uncurled his clawed toes and shuffled sideways along the branch.

'I won't be long,' Fleur told him breezily. She knew nothing about the forest, so she decided not to venture too far in – just skirt the edge of the trees and see what she could find. Maybe there would be some creepers or vines that she could take back and use for lashing together the wood that would form the platform for their raft.

Time's whizzing by, she thought as she climbed the hill and entered the shade of the tree canopy. *Soon we'll have been cast away on Dolphin Island for a whole week and who knows how much longer it'll be before we even see another plane? We could be here for ages.*

Fleur shivered as she went into the silent forest. It was colder here. The trees were tall and the leaf canopy never let in any sunlight. Besides, she still didn't know what lived in the shadows. Were eyes secretly watching her? Was there a snake waiting in the undergrowth to rear up and bite? She shuddered again as silence surrounded her like a muggy cloak.

For a moment Fleur was tempted to turn around and hurry back to camp empty-handed, but the sight of long creepers looped between high branches made her stay. Looking more closely as her eyes adjusted to the dim light, she saw vines entwined around broad trunks, twisting upwards into the branches – stems that looked strong and flexible enough to be used as rope if only Fleur could detach them from the trunks. This would mean stepping through thick undergrowth and running the risk of disturbing those hidden creatures. Was it worth it?

Once more she paused to gather her courage. She stared up at branches swathed in creepers then down at exposed, gnarled roots stretching in every direction. Yes, she would manage it by stepping from root to root, she decided. That way she would stay clear of any dangers hidden in the undergrowth. And there was a vine clinging to a trunk about ten metres away – easy enough to reach if she planned out her route.

So she stepped up on to a root as thick as her arm that arched clear of the ground. Once she had stretched her arms wide like a tightrope walker and was sure of her balance, she edged to a second, thicker root, then a third, until she came to the vine she wanted. Reaching it, she tugged at the bendy stem, finding just enough space to squeeze her fingers between it and the smooth bark of the tree. She tugged again and managed to prise a longer section free, exposing beetles and spiders as she kept on freeing the vine. 'Sorry,' Fleur muttered to the insects as she robbed them of their habitats.

After five minutes of careful tugging ten centimetres at a time, she'd finally freed a long, unbroken section of vine and brought it tumbling down.

Enough for now, Fleur decided, gathering her vine, looping it over her shoulder and slowly retracing her steps along the tree roots to the edge of the forest. The tips of her fingers were sore and when she took off her hat, she shook off fallen leaves and wriggling caterpillars that had collected in the brim.

'Time to take this lot home,' she told the cockatoo

still perched on his branch overlooking the spring. She picked up the water bottles and followed her familiar route down the cliff, not even looking out for new species of butterflies, beetles or spiders. The truth was, she couldn't wait to get back and see the look on everyone's faces when she told them where she'd been!

*

Alfie and Mia arrived home with their bamboo canes at the same time as Fleur appeared with her creeper. They found their mum fixing the leaky roof with more palm leaves and their dad sitting in the doorway carefully unravelling the blue rope that Mia had found on the beach. A good fire blazed and a breakfast smell of roasted coconut filled their nostrils.

'I've been in the forest!' Fleur declared.

'We found loads of bamboo!' Mia cried, puffing out her chest and high-fiving Katie and James.

Fleur flung her coil of creeper on to the ground. 'Did you hear? I've been in the actual forest all by myself. Creepy-crawlies, snakes, scorpions – whoo!'

'Yes, but look at our brilliant bamboo canes.' Alfie was so pleased with himself and Mia that he laid the canes out then stood back to admire them.

'Whoa, this is not a competition!' James turned to Katie. 'I may be biased but wouldn't you say that we have *three* amazing kids?' he said with a grin when he saw the result of their morning's work.

His smiling wife agreed. 'You've had to take on a lot, especially with your dad not able to do much. We're very proud of you.'

Fleur, Alfie and Mia looked at each other and grinned. Underneath their deep suntans they glowed with pride.

'Well done for venturing into the forest, Fleur.' James picked up the length of creeper that she'd brought back. 'I knew we didn't have nearly enough rope to hold the raft together, so this liana is exactly what we need.'

'Liana?' Mia echoed.

'It means jungle creeper,' Alfie explained. 'What about our bamboo? Will we need more?'

'Definitely,' Katie confirmed.

An eager Alfie and Mia were about to set off again when their mum stopped them.

'Hold it. Have breakfast first and take a rest. Then you can go back.'

So, as they tucked into coconut chunks and drank coconut milk from their plastic mugs followed by big gulps of water from the bottles, Alfie, Fleur and Mia discussed the best way to tie the canes together and attach them to the containers.

'Do we need to check that the containers will float?' Alfie wanted to know.

'They will,' his mum assured him, 'especially since we're able to use these nice, light canes. Listen, everyone – here's what we're going to do after breakfast. Fleur – you and I will stay here and make a start on the platform. Alfie and Mia, you'll go back for more bamboo.'

'What about me?' James asked.

'You already know the answer to that – you're staying stay right where you are until your ribs heal,' Katie said. 'So kick back and let us take the strain.'

*

'It's working!' Fleur said as she started to wind a length of liana around two canes held in place by her mum. The creeper felt just like tough string – you could bend

138

it and knot it then move on to the next cane and so on.

Her happy voice followed Alfie and Mia down the beach as they set off for a second load of bamboo. It seemed to them that at this rate the raft would be finished before sunset.

As always, Mia scampered on ahead, crossing the rocks and jumping down into the neighbouring cove then running up the beach to the clump of bamboos. She waited impatiently for Alfie to arrive and hopped from one foot to the other until he'd begun to hack away at the canes.

'Timber!' he cried as the first one fell to the ground with a loud rustle.

Mia seized it, stripped the leaves from the tall stem, then grabbed the next one, not stopping for breath until they had another big bundle to carry back to camp in triumph.

'Slow down!' Alfie pleaded as Mia gathered the canes together. Once more he was tired and sweating from the effort.

She took no notice. 'Let's go!' she cried, picking up her end of the bundle.

On they strode, out across the sand with the hot sun beating down, until, just before they reached the headland, Mia suddenly felt her legs go wobbly and she dropped the canes, sank to her knees and toppled forward.

Alfie watched her land face-down on the hot sand. He gasped, ran to her and turned her on to her back. 'What happened?' he cried.

Mia stared up at him with a dazed expression. Everything – Alfie's face, his hat and the wispy clouds in the sky – looked shimmery and her head was spinning.

'Heat stroke,' Alfie decided. He knew this was serious. 'Too much sun and not enough to drink.' He began to panic, tearing off his hat and flapping it over Mia's face, then, abandoning the canes, he dragged her down to the water's edge and began to splash her face.

'Mia, wake up!' he cried.

'Hey!' Mia protested when she felt the cold shower on her cheeks. She shook her head and tried to stand up but her legs still wouldn't work.

Alfie kneeled beside her and wondered what to do next. He needn't have worried – within seconds, Pearl and Stormy were on the scene, rising to the surface like twin lifeguards ploughing steadily through the water. They stopped close to the shore and waited for Alfie to work out the rescue plan.

'I get it!' he declared. 'Mia – Stormy and Pearl have come to help. They know you can't make it home over the rocks.'

'How can they help?' Mia croaked through dry lips.

'They can carry you back to our beach. OK?'

Mia nodded slowly. Her head was starting to clear and she could make out the shapes of the two dolphins.

'Good, let's do it.' Alfie picked Mia up and carried her into the water towards Pearl and Stormy. When they were waist-deep, the combination of a breeze and the cool water had revived her a little so she reached out to take hold of Stormy's fin with her right hand and Pearl's with her left.

'Sure you're OK?' Alfie checked. 'You need to hold on, you know. Don't fall off, whatever you do.'

Another nod from Mia gave her dolphin rescuers the signal they needed to set off, gently at first then gathering speed as they reached the headland. She felt them surge through the calm water, their smooth bodies to either side, their heads clear of the surface.

'Hold your chin up and hang on tight!' Alfie called as Pearl and Stormy carried Mia out of sight.

Chapter Twelve

DRINK MORE WATER! Fleur wrote giant letters in the sand.

'Never mind planes – aliens could see that from outer space,' Alfie laughed. It was late in the afternoon and Mia was feeling much better since Pearl and Stormy had seen her safely home.

The two dolphins had swum close to shore and stayed there with Mia until Fleur had glanced up from her task of building the raft. She'd seen Mia sitting in the water with Pearl and Stormy and had hurried to tell her off for messing around with the dolphins instead of bringing back more bamboo.

'I couldn't help it. I felt dizzy and fell down,' Mia had explained in a hurt voice, her knees wobbly as she stood up out of the water. 'I'm really, really thirsty.'

Fleur had helped her to stand and walked her slowly up the beach. 'Where's Alfie?'

'He's bringing the bamboo.'

Sure enough, as Mia and Fleur had reached the shade of the palm trees and Mia had been given water by an anxious Katie, Alfie had appeared on the eastern headland. He'd shouldered all the canes and carried them over the rocks, bending forward under their weight. Fleur had run to help him. In the end, Mia, Alfie and the bamboo canes had all reached home in one piece.

'By hook or by crook,' James had commented.

'We all know we must drink more water!' was Katie's new mantra.

So it was later in the day, when the fierce heat of the sun was fading, that Fleur went on to the beach and wrote the giant reminder in the wet sand. DRINK MORE WATER! By now, the platform was almost finished – a rectangle of canes neatly bound together with rope and liana, roughly two metres long and one and a half metres wide.

Mia turned to her dad. 'Now can we have a go on the

raft?' she demanded for the fifth time that afternoon.

'Someone's definitely feeling better,' James said from inside the shelter, where he'd gone for another rest. He left it to Alfie to give Mia the reasons why not.

'Number one – we still have to tie the platform to the containers. Number two – it'll soon be dark.'

'Spoilsport,' Mia grumbled.

'Number three – we need more drinking water,' Fleur added. 'Number four – more firewood.' Here on Dolphin Island there were always jobs to do.

So Alfie went off to fetch water while Fleur and Mia scouted in George's cave for wood.

 'For the fire,' Fleur explained to her favourite gecko. 'You know – sparks and flames, all the stuff you don't like.'

'You can come back with us or you can stay here with the bats,' Mia added.

George didn't move. He just looked at them collecting branches and driftwood in his wise, wide-eyed way.

They reached base at the same time as Alfie, who arrived with bottles of water and a big surprise.

'Jackfruit for supper!' he announced, depositing a knobbly, yellowish fruit the size and shape of a rugby ball on the grass outside the shelter. He'd found it lying on the ground at the edge of the forest and, even though he'd only seen it cut into chunks on market stalls, he'd recognized what it was. He didn't know much about how or where it grew – only that it was delicious. 'Pass me a knife, someone.'

'It tastes like pineapple,' Fleur decided, once the jackfruit had been carved up and shared between them. Her face was flushed from the fire, her mouth full of pulpy, chewy fruit.

'Apple,' was Katie's verdict.

'Banana,' James insisted.

'Mango,' Alfie said, stirring the fire and making sparks fly.

'Yum!' Mia didn't care what it tasted like – she held out her hand for more.

*

Day 5 dawned clear and calm. Fleur crawled out of the shelter at daybreak to find that the sea was as still as a millpond. Waves broke with no more than a shallow ripple on the shore. 'Wake up, everyone – it's a perfect day for rafting,' she announced as she piled more wood on to the dwindling fire.

Alfie and Mia were awake in a flash and they soon joined Fleur to work out the best way to attach the containers to the raft.

'I was figuring it out before I went to sleep,' Alfie said. 'The containers have got handles so we can thread a piece of liana through the hole, make a knot, then tie one to each corner of the platform.' Working as he talked, Alfie showed Fleur and Mia how to finish the raft. 'We want to keep the containers tucked under the platform. That way, the raft will float clear of the water and we'll be able to keep everything dry.'

'Can we bring Monkey back this time?' Mia asked. She stood aside to watch Fleur and Alfie finish the knots then turn the raft the right way up to set it down on the sand.

'It depends,' Fleur replied. 'We need useful stuff – tins of food, towels, more rope.'

'Fishing nets, insect screens, first-aid kit ...' The list went on inside Alfie's head.

Fleur looked down at the raft and then out to sea. She saw that the tide was going out and judged that it would take about fifteen minutes to paddle from the shore to their wrecked boat. 'We need to get a move on before the tide turns. Let's carry the raft down to the water and find out if it actually floats!'

So, with Alfie at the front and Mia and Fleur at the back, they picked it up and ran with it to the water's edge, with Katie staying behind to search for other things they might need.

'It's nice and light.' Alfie seemed happy with the raft's construction.

'But will it be strong enough to take our weight?' Fleur wondered as they waded in to waist-height.

Gingerly they lowered the raft on to the water and held their breaths.

'Hurray – it floats!' Mia cried.

'It floats!' Fleur and Alfie echoed, looking at each other with relieved smiles.

They didn't notice the raft get caught in a gentle current and swirl lazily away from them. Alfie had to lunge after it and catch hold of one corner. He drew it back and held it steady. 'Mia, you're the lightest – you try first.'

With a whoop of excitement, Mia threw herself belly-down on to the floating platform. She landed off-centre. The raft tipped violently to one side, throwing her off. 'Yuck!' She came up spluttering with a mouth full of seawater.

'Gently,' Fleur explained before she showed Mia how to do it, easing herself on to the raft while Alfie and Mia held it level. 'Like this.'

Fleur lay belly-down and started to use her hands to paddle forward. 'See – it does feel like I'm on a lilo, only not so comfy,' she told the others, aware now that their mum was striding down the beach carrying life vests and two flat pieces of wood salvaged from George's cave.

'These planks are for oars,' Katie told Fleur and Alfie as they put on their vests. 'Alfie, you sit on the left side. Fleur, you're on the right. OK, I'll hold the raft level while you both get into position. That's right – you need to kneel up so you're able to paddle. Mia, you stay here with me.'

'But that's not fair – I want to go too!' Mia protested. 'I want to find Monkey.'

'Not this time.' Katie gave her reasons calmly and firmly. 'There's only room for two people, and Dad or I would be too heavy. Fleur and Alfie are older than you – you'll get a turn later.'

With their mum in this kind of mood, even Mia knew there was no point in arguing.

'Most important of all,' Katie continued, 'do not – I repeat, do not take any risks. If you get out there and you find for any reason that it's not safe to go on board, turn right around and come back. Nothing on *Merlin* is worth putting yourselves in danger for – understand?'

'OK,' Alfie agreed and tried to ignore a flutter of fear around his heart.

'Don't worry, Mum – we'll be fine.' Fleur knew that it wouldn't be long before the tide turned and she was eager to start paddling.

So Fleur and Alfie set off across the calm water towards *Merlin* who was still wallowing on her side, caught fast on her twin peaks of rock.

'Take it in turns to paddle,' Fleur told Alfie, pushing

her oar through the crystal-clear water. 'Me then you, me then you ...'

They soon got into a rhythm, balanced on one knee, the other foot out in front to steady themselves, making good progress on their flimsy bamboo raft – 'Me – you. Me – you. Me – you.' – in a straight line towards *Merlin*. Above their heads, the sky was blue and empty; below them the sea swarmed with marine life – shoals of black and white parrot fish, a solitary, predatory tarpon and scary clusters of white, pulsating jellyfish.

Fleur and Alfie fixed all their concentration on reaching the boat. They didn't notice the dolphin pod quietly rise to the surface beyond the wreck and keep silent watch.

'Almost there,' Alfie muttered. He could hear water lapping at *Merlin*'s exposed hull and see thick blades of sea grass caught in her mangled propeller. He didn't admit it to Fleur, but the sight of the boat lying on her side made him feel scared all over again. It still reminded him too much of the storm – the heaving waves, the howling winds and the moment he'd been thrown overboard. *That's stupid*, he told himself. *The*

*sea's as calm as anything. There isn't going to be
another storm.*

But he was relieved when they reached the boat
safely and Fleur handed him her paddle. 'Can you stay
close so I can throw things down to you?' she asked.

'Don't you want me to come aboard with you?'

'No. You need to stay on the raft to catch stuff.'
Fleur knew what to expect on board – she'd done it
before, so she didn't mind sliding from the raft into the
water then swimming a few strokes to the rock where
she found footholds to haul herself up level with
Merlin. 'It's a bit harder this time,' she called down to
Alfie. 'The boat's higher out of the water. I'll have to go
around the far side to climb on deck.'

Seeing her disappear from view and remembering
their mum's warning, he shouted back. 'Make sure
it's safe!'

'I will. I'm in the cockpit. I've found two hammocks
and some fishing nets in the storage cupboard, plus a
spare sail and lots of rigging. Can you paddle the raft
round here to fetch them?'

With his heart in his mouth, Alfie kneeled in the

centre of the raft and made his way slowly around the wreck to find Fleur balanced on the sloping deck, laden with the useful things she'd salvaged. His raft rocked unsteadily in the waves lapping against the hull.

'Ready?' Fleur asked. She knelt down and let the spare sail billow free, hoping that Alfie would be able to catch one end. 'OK, good. Let's use the sail as a chute. Here come the hammocks!'

Alfie saw them slide down the sail and felt them thud into his chest. He kept his balance and eased them on to the platform.

'Now the fishing nets and the rigging,' Fleur called.

Alfie did the same as before. The nets and a coil of polyester rope were safely stowed at his feet and his confidence was growing. 'What now?'

But as he spoke, there was a sudden grating sound and Fleur felt *Merlin* shift under her feet. The sensation scared her into retreating from the edge of the deck, back towards the cockpit. 'My weight must have made her tip!' she yelled.

'Remember – Mum said don't take risks!'

'I know. But I haven't been down below yet. I was

planning to fetch the first-aid kit and more cooking things – maybe Mia's Monkey if I can find him.' Again Fleur heard the same scraping sound and this time the boat definitely settled further on to her side.

'Don't do it!' Alfie's heart was in his mouth and he was desperate for her not to go down the companionway. What if she went below and got trapped? 'It's not worth it.'

Fleur grimaced. Down in the cabins she heard waves wash against the lightweight partition walls and a glance down the companionway ladder told her that the water level was high. 'OK – you win,' she called reluctantly. 'I'm on my way.'

So Alfie prayed that Fleur would keep her footing on the slippery, sloping deck and only started to breathe again when he saw her scramble off *Merlin* on to the rock. Then he came as close to her as he dared and held his breath again as she jumped into the sea and struck out towards the raft.

'I'm way out of my depth. How do I get back on without capsizing you?' Fleur's upturned, puzzled face bobbed in the sparkling sea. She trod water while she tried to work it out.

'Oh yeah, you're right. We never thought of that,' Alfie realized. He looked at the shore, to where their mum and Mia waited anxiously.

'OK, so I'll swim back,' Fleur decided. It would be hard work because she'd be going against the tide but she reckoned she could do it. 'How about you? Can you paddle by yourself?'

Gamely Alfie nodded. He set off slowly for shore with his precious cargo while Fleur swam breaststroke beside him. However, they hadn't gone far – perhaps about ten metres – when they found they had their usual company. Three dolphins nosed their way to the surface. Pearl and Stormy whistled and clicked out a greeting then swam smoothly behind Alfie, who felt the raft suddenly surge forward. He looked back to see his sleek grey helpers pushing him with their rounded snouts, looking up at him and noisily blowing air out of their nostrils.

'Wow – dolphin power!' Alfie cried out in delight to Fleur who was also hitching a ride.

She waved at him and swung a leg over Jazz's back.

'Am I glad to see you!' she told him.

Jazz smacked his tail flukes on the surface and snaked his strong body through the raft's frothy wake.

And this was how Alfie and Fleur reached the shore within seconds, thanks to their dolphin friends. Clapping and shouting, Mia ran into the sea to give Stormy a hug while Katie waded in and carried Fleur's salvaged haul to safety.

'Thanks a lot,' Fleur told Jazz. She felt exhilarated by the speed of their journey. 'But you realize Alfie and I were OK – we could've done it by ourselves.'

Jazz ignored her. He nuzzled close and chirped loudly for attention.

'That's right – we could.' Alfie stroked Pearl.

Pearl smiled at him then flapped her flippers and gave a low whistle.

'We could!' Fleur and Alfie protested loudly.

'But you didn't need to,' Mia pointed out as she frolicked happily with Stormy.

Then, after a few minutes and as if in response to a signal unheard by the human ear, the three young dolphins clapped their jaws together and lined up in a row. In perfect unison they performed a backwards flip, landing with a slap and a splash that soaked Mia, Alfie and Fleur.

Goodbye for now, they seemed to say, as they lifted their flippers clear of the water in a gesture of farewell. Then off they swam at top speed, fins slicing through the calm water out to sea – their good deed done.

Chapter Thirteen

'There's never a dull moment on a desert island,' James grumbled at Fleur and Alfie later that same day. 'Here am I, trying to have a quiet kip, and you two come, disrupting my beauty sleep.'

'We know, Dad.' Fleur helped him to stand up while Alfie carried the life vests he was using as cushions out of the shelter. 'We're sorry but you have to move.'

'Ouch. Ooch! Ouch!' Their unshaven, bleary-eyed dad creaked and groaned his way out. 'What's going on?'

'Home improvements,' Fleur explained. She sat him down under a palm tree and made him comfy. 'We've learned a lot about how to make a better shelter since we first got here – we've decided we want to build it on stilts with a wooden frame and a bamboo floor.'

'Come again?' James shook his head in disbelief.

'Isn't that a teeny bit over-the-top?'

'No – it's to make sure the sandflies can't get at us and we don't get flooded out when it rains.' A determined Alfie went back to the job he'd been doing before. He stripped leaves from the sturdiest canes left over from building the raft and laid them out in a rectangle on the floor of the shelter.

'I give in,' James said with a sigh and a groan. 'But it drives me crazy that I can't lend a hand.'

'Never mind, Dad – you can be the project manager,' Fleur suggested with a cheeky grin. Her next task was to carry the sail that she'd salvaged from *Merlin* on to the beach, spread it out and see how much cloth they had to make a new, waterproof roof for the shelter. She was happy with what she saw. 'It's huge – I reckon we'll even have some left over for other things. How are you getting on, Alfie?'

Inside the shelter, Alfie was using his full weight to shove short stakes deep into the sandy soil, making sure that they were upright and evenly spaced. 'Good, thanks. These are the stilts. Next we make a frame and tie it to them – that's the start of our raised floor.'

'It's a lot of work,' James warned him. 'You're bound to need more bamboo.'

'And more lianas,' Fleur agreed. 'Mum and Mia are fetching them right now.'

Leaning back against the tree trunk, James gave a wry smile. 'I've said it before – I'm impressed. Who'd have believed you kids would learn so much so fast about how to survive on a desert island?'

Fleur laughed and twisted her hair up into the crown of her hat. 'Are you still proud of us?'

'Totally. We're less than a week in and you're already seasoned castaways, fetching water, building fires, fishing, not to mention making a raft and paddling out to sea – while all I can do is sit on my backside and wait for my pesky rib to heal.'

Fleur broke off from measuring the sail and went to sit beside him. 'Don't worry,' she said, putting an arm around his shoulder. His glum face with its stubbly beard made her smile. 'I'll tell you a joke to cheer you up.'

James grimaced and shook his head. 'Ouch, no. Laughing is agony. I mean it, Fleury – this is serious.'

Doing her best to keep a straight face, Fleur changed

the subject. 'We'll soon have a new floor and roof, then we'll be able to use handy tree trunks to support the walls and string up a hammock for you to sleep in. How comfy will that be?'

'And guess what – we're having poached eggs!' Mia raced up the beach and burst in on them. Carrying her upturned hat, she almost tripped over the pile of canes stacked up outside the shelter.

Following close behind, Katie steadied her and kept the contents of the hat in place. 'Careful, Mia – at this rate those eggs will have to be scrambled, not poached.'

Alfie, Fleur and James looked in amazement inside Mia's hat to see six pure white eggs nestling in the crown.

'I found gulls' nests on the cliff!' she cried. 'I asked Mum if I could fetch the eggs and she said yes. We can cook them for tea!'

*

Improvements to the shelter took the rest of Friday and all of Saturday – Days 5 and 6 on Dolphin Island. By sunset on Saturday, after lots of effort and a few setbacks, the new canvas roof was cut to shape and securely tied in place with strong lianas. The raised floor was finished at last.

'Good job!' James gave his verdict. 'I admit I had my doubts, but I was wrong. This is luxury compared with what we had before.'

'Time to celebrate!' Katie declared. 'Let's have a feast.'

That afternoon, Mia had collected more eggs from the cliff and another jackfruit from the edge of the forest. Alfie and Fleur had spent an hour out on the headland and Alfie had finally caught a red snapper in his new net. Soon the fish was gutted and grilled, the eggs scrambled in the pan and the fruit dessert cut up into juicy chunks.

'This is certainly living the high life,' Katie said between happy mouthfuls. She smiled at Mia sitting cross-legged by the fire in her exotic hat and Supergirl cape, at Alfie tucking into the fish he'd caught, his face lit up by flickering flames, and at Fleur gazing hopefully out to sea. 'Do you see any of your dolphins?' she asked.

Fleur shook her head. 'They haven't visited us at all today,' she reported. The sun had already sunk below the horizon and the light was pearly grey. A fresh wind whipped the surface of the silvery sea into small peaks of white foam.

'Maybe they went deep-sea fishing again,' Katie suggested as she stirred the dying embers and bright sparks flew up into the air then faded to nothing. 'Don't worry – they'll be back soon.'

Then Alfie came up with another theory. 'Remember we told them we could have paddled the raft back from *Merlin* without them? We said we didn't really need them. Well, maybe they stayed away on purpose because they want us to *prove* it.'

'No, Alfie – I don't think so,' James argued. 'Bottle-nose dolphins may be smart, but not that smart!'

Alfie gave Fleur and Mia a piercing look. Their eyes reflected flickering firelight. Were they thinking what he was thinking – that Pearl, Jazz and Stormy were not only beautiful and graceful, speedy, strong and playful, but they also belonged to the most super-intelligent species in the entire world?

'Oh, yes they are!' Alfie, Mia and Fleur chorused with one voice.

'Pearl always knows what I'm thinking,' Alfie insisted.

'When there's a problem, Jazz works out what to do,' Fleur pointed out.

'Stormy plays with me when I'm sad,' Mia added wistfully.

Katie leaned over and squeezed her youngest daughter's hand. 'Are you sad now because of Monkey, little Mia?'

Mia held her head up and stuck out her chin. 'No, because I know Stormy will find a ship and lead it to Dolphin Island to rescue us,' she said.

Katie squeezed her hand again then glanced uncertainly at Fleur, James and Alfie. Embers shifted and sparks flew. 'Yes, I suppose he might,' she said softly. 'With dolphins anything is possible.'

*

That night everyone slept well. James and Katie snoozed contentedly in hammocks while for the first time Fleur, Alfie and Mia lay on thin mattresses made from sailcloth stuffed with leaves.

At sunrise Fleur was woken by a tickling sensation on her arm. She opened her eyes to see George planted squarely on her shoulder, carefully checking out the inside of the new, improved shelter for tasty spiders and beetles. She lay a while, quietly enjoying a close view of the pale, scaly skin under the gecko's chin, the suction pads on his toes and his staring, bright yellow eyes.

Then Mia woke up and turned the silent world upside down. Up in the blink of an eye, she jammed her hat on her head and scrambled over Fleur to reach the doorway, kicking Alfie's head by mistake while a panicky George fled to the safety of James's hammock.

'Hey!' Alfie objected. 'What's the hurry?'

'Sorry, Alfie!' Mia muttered on her way out. Then she remembered the calendar stick and crawled back inside. There was more chaos as she searched for her piece of charcoal.

'– Not!' Alfie groaned.

'– Am!'

'– Not!'

'I guess it's time to get up,' Fleur sighed. She rolled off her mattress and made her way outside to stoke the fire. 'Sshh!' she warned Mia and Alfie. 'Mum and Dad are still asleep. Who's coming for a swim?'

'Me!' Mia shot out of the shelter on to the beach.

'Not me,' Alfie replied, turning over and trying to get back to sleep.

So the girls walked down to the sea, noticing the usual gulls and pelicans perched on the rocks and a pair of white, long-legged birds with curved yellow bills standing in shallow water and pecking at tangles of seaweed. When Mia and Fleur drew near, the ibis spread their wings and flew off.

'Brrr – the water's cold,' Mia complained when she waded in. But then she saw a big conch shell roll towards her on a small wave and, forgetting her complaint, she ran to pick it up. She held it in both hands and shook it hard.

'You're right – it is.' The sea was definitely cooler than normal, Fleur realized. She looked out to where *Merlin* was wedged on the rocks and beyond that to a bank of light clouds gathering to the east – the direction where bad weather always built up. 'We'd better have a quick swim,' she told Mia. 'Then get back to tell the others that it's going to pour down – again!' Bracing herself to plunge into the next wave, Fleur swam underwater and came up twenty metres from where Mia stood ankle-deep, her mouth open and pointing out to sea.

Wringing salty water from her hair, Fleur followed Mia's pointing finger. 'What?' she asked.

'There's a ship!' Mia gasped, jumping for joy. 'Ship! Ship!' It was yesterday's dream come true. 'Honestly, I'm not making it up. There it is!'

Fleur looked again and this time she made out a small white shape on the horizon. As she screwed up her eyes and made out a faraway ship, her heart leaped. Which direction was it taking and would it head their way? 'Let's tell the others!' she hissed.

They ran up the beach, shouting as they went.

'Everyone, wake up!' Mia yelled in a high voice.

'We have to build up the fire, make lots of smoke!' Fleur seized branches and piled them on to the flames.

Alfie emerged from the shelter rubbing his eyes. 'Are you serious?'

'Yes! Yes!' Fleur pointed to the horizon. 'We've waited a whole week for this. See for yourself.'

Slowly the white blob on the horizon came into

focus and Alfie's heart skipped a beat. It was a big boat with lots of decks – the type that sailed from port to port with thousands of tourists on board. 'Cruise ship,' he muttered.

'Don't just stand there – help me!' Fleur cried as she threw more wood on to the fire. The higher they built it, the more chance they had of the ship being able to spot their flames and smoke.

Frantically Mia and Alfie lent a hand and by the time Katie and James came out of the shelter, the hungry fire roared and shot up tongues of yellow flame high in the sky.

'Make them notice us!' Mia begged her mum and dad. 'Make them come!'

Katie looked in alarm at the dangerous flames curling up towards the tree canopy. 'That's enough,' she warned. 'If we make it any bigger, we'll set fire to the whole island.'

Fleur, Alfie and Mia stopped feeding the fire to watch and pray as the ship sailed steadily on, taking with it their wistful thoughts of friends and family on the far side of the world.

'It's no good. It's the same as the plane – too far away.' Shaking his head, Alfie was the first to back away from the fire and walk slowly down to the shore. He pictured the ship's passengers sunbathing or playing deck games, not even looking up from their books and newspapers to notice tiny Dolphin Island as they sailed calmly on.

Soon Fleur joined him. Smoke had got into her eyes and made them sting. 'They can't see us,' she murmured, her spirits sinking even lower than when their fire had gone out and the plane had ignored her message in the sand.

Alfie gave a deep sigh. 'Mia had the right idea – this is when we need the dolphins to grab the ship's attention.'

'Even then ...' Fleur's voice trailed away. People on a cruise ship sailing tropical waters loved to watch a pod of dolphins playing in the wide, foaming wake or riding the swelling bow wave. They took videos of them leaping clear of the water, spinning in the air and diving back down. But no way would the captain change course to follow them. And who on board would tear their gaze away from dolphins to gaze across a wide, empty ocean? No – it was a forlorn hope to think that anyone would spot a thin trail of smoke on a tiny, unnamed island in the middle of an azure sea.

'So I guess we'll have to stay here a bit longer,' Alfie said as the ship sailed steadily on. He sneaked a sideways look at Fleur. 'You're not crying, are you?'

'I've got smoke in my eyes, that's all. Why, are you?'

Alfie sniffed and wiped his sweaty face with the back of his hand. 'No way.'

'So you don't mind?'

'Staying on Dolphin Island?' He did his best to look on the bright side. 'No. Think about it – we won't have to go back to school in September. We can do what we like when we like. It's cool here.'

Fleur watched the ship sail on into the west. 'Yes. And later today we can sail the raft out to *Merlin* and fetch more stuff.'

Alfie turned away from the departing cruise ship and looked uneasily towards the clouds in the east. 'Not if the wind gets up and it starts to rain again,' he warned. 'No one will be going anywhere if we get another storm.'

Chapter Fourteen

All morning the clouds built up in the east. The air was still and humid. There was no wind.

'Maybe this time the storm will miss us.' A hopeful Katie stood on the headland looking down at Alfie and Fleur who fished in shallow water with their nets. 'Those clouds haven't moved all morning.'

Spotting a nice fat grouper lurking under a rock, Fleur swished her net through the water and tried to scoop it up. The fish was too quick – it flicked its tail and swam away. 'Anyway, I hope it doesn't rain before we catch our supper,' she muttered.

'We've got more eggs and coconut to be going on with. And plenty of water.' Her mum had made sure they'd stocked up with essentials in case the storm broke but still she seemed anxious. 'I'm going to scout around for firewood,' she told Fleur and Alfie. 'It's best to be prepared.'

Like Fleur, Alfie didn't want to give up and go back to the shelter until they'd caught some fish. 'We'll stay here,' he told his mum.

'Come straight back if the weather changes,' she warned as she picked her way down from the rocks and went on scouting for driftwood.

Fleur and Alfie promised they would.

Then Fleur spotted the same grouper busy feeding on silversides. 'Here, fishy, fishy!' she coaxed. With another swoop of her net she trapped him against a rock and scooped him up. He was out of the water, wriggling in her net, then out again with a sudden flip and twist of his fat, grey body, plopping back into the sea and swimming away. Fleur gave a disgusted grunt.

Alfie looked up at the sky. Thin wisps of white cloud were drifting overhead and he thought he felt a drop of rain in the wind. He waded out of the water on to the shore. 'OK, I give in. Let's go.'

'Five more minutes,' Fleur muttered. She darted her net towards a small shoal of silver fish that sheltered under some rocks.

So Alfie trudged up the beach alone. The wind was growing stronger and rain was falling. Dark grey clouds covered the sun.

'Where's Fleur?' Mia asked when he reached the shelter.

'Still fishing.' Wearily he laid down his net and went inside.

James looked up from repairs he was making to the metal grate they used for cooking. 'Tell your sister to come quickly,' he told Mia, who ran down the beach in the rain. 'And you too, Mia – I want you both back here.'

A gust of wind whipped Mia's hat from her head and tumbled it across the sand. She chased it to the water's edge, picked it up and jammed it back on. 'Dad says you have to come back!' she yelled at Fleur.

Fleur held up her empty net. The usually clear water had turned a murky brown, making it impossible to see any fish. 'OK, I'm on my way!' She joined Mia on the beach and they paused to look out to sea.

'No dolphins,' Mia sighed.

'No – wait a second – yes!' Fleur spotted the welcome

sight of curved fins circling in choppy waters around *Merlin*'s rocks then heading across the bay towards them.

'Cool!' Mia's face lit up. Without thinking about her dad's order to go straight back to camp, she waded deeper, only to feel a cold current swirl around her legs and drag her off her feet.

'Hold on!' Fleur fought to stay upright, struggling to catch hold of Mia's hand and drag her back. Wind battered them and churned up the surface of the water, making it hard to see if the dolphins were still there.

But yes – Jazz swam up and nudged her with his snout then Stormy surged clear of the water and whistled. Pearl brought up the rear, swimming in a tight circle around them all. They seemed agitated, their clicks more rapid than usual, their whistles more shrill. And no wonder, because the waves were growing bigger every second, rolling in with more and more force, breaking over Fleur and Mia and knocking them over. On their hands and knees they scrambled for the shore and when they reached safety and turned, another dolphin had appeared – an adult with a pearly pink underbelly, calling loudly to the young ones.

Fleur held Mia tightly by the hand. 'It's Marina,' she murmured. 'She's worried about Pearl. The water's too rough – she wants them to leave.'

Sure enough, Marina swiftly took charge. As the waves crashed and a fierce wind drove dark clouds towards Dolphin Island, she rounded up Pearl, Stormy and Jazz and swiftly pushed them away from the shore. Fleur and Mia caught glimpses of them between the breaking waves, swimming strongly but being swept off course by currents, disappearing below the surface for more than a minute then coming up again, this time much too close to *Merlin*'s rocks.

Mia gasped and put her hands over her eyes, not daring to look. Fleur swallowed back her fear for the young dolphins. Sensible Marina was there to guide them – she would steer them clear of the rocks and lead them out to sea.

'Mia, Fleur – come here now!' James's faint voice reached them. He was standing by the fire with cupped hands, yelling with all his might.

Rain lashed down. The wind howled as it ripped

through the palm trees. Waves crashed on to the headlands, sending a wall of spray high into the air.

There was no sign of the dolphins out by *Merlin*'s rocks – only wind and mist and mountainous waves.

*

The family spent a miserable hour hunched inside their shelter, looking out at the raging storm.

'This is as bad as any we've seen,' James muttered.

'Yes, and it's lasting longer,' Katie agreed. Tropical storms didn't come much worse than this but at least they were protected from the worst of it by staying in the shelter.

Fleur, Mia and Alfie's faces were lit by a sudden flash of lightning that forked through the blue-black sky. Their eyes were wide with fear.

For their sakes, their dad tried to sound cheerful. 'Luckily the new roof doesn't let in water. I bet we're all glad about that.'

'Not yet, it doesn't,' Katie murmured as she felt the wind tear at the canvas and heard the rain lash down.

'And we've still got fire.'

'Just.'

Fleur crept to the doorway and peered out. Her mum was right – the fire was struggling to stay alight. It hissed and collapsed under the force of the rain and she knew for sure that before long it would go out like it did before. 'Alfie, Mia, come on – let's build it up.'

Braving the wind, they stepped out into the storm to feed the fire. Needle-sharp rain stung the skin on their shoulders and backs as they bent to pick up driftwood and throw it on to the hissing flames but soon the pile was gone.

'There's some stashed away in George's cave.' Fleur didn't hesitate – she leaned into the wind and set off across the beach to fetch more wood, followed by Alfie and Mia. Fire came before everything – that was the rule. It didn't matter how hard it rained or how often lightning forked across the sky and thunder rolled, the fire must not be allowed to go out.

So they reached the cave and stumbled inside to catch their breath before they started lugging wood back to camp. Mia sat on the ground, drew her knees to her chin and shivered. Alfie coughed then pushed wet hair from his forehead. Fleur breathed in deeply

and looked in vain for George on his usual ledge.

But there was no time to worry about him – the fire had to be saved. All three seized as much wood as they could carry and prepared to stagger back out into the storm. They were met by a blast of wind and a wall of spray from waves thundering on to the beach. Beyond the spray, a dark green sea swelled and swirled, crashing against headlands with a deafening roar. And then, further out again, Fleur, Alfie and Mia caught

glimpses of stricken *Merlin* caught on the black rocks,
battered by waves that crashed and broke over her
then sucked away, only to rise and crash again.

Lightning flashed – a fork that split the sky in two.
And in that instant the children saw something they'd
never imagined would happen, even in their worst
nightmares. The sea lifted *Merlin* from her rocks as if
their poor boat was a toy – lifted her and carried her
free, turned her hull uppermost then dashed her back

against the rock, shattering the damaged vessel and snapping her clean in two.

Alfie, Fleur and Mia watched in horror as *Merlin* broke apart. They saw the waves crash down on the rock and when the spray cleared there was no sign of their boat – only a large circle of swirling foam to mark where she had been.

Their stomachs churned. *Merlin* was gone. She was broken in two and sinking down amongst the corals and sea grass, down and down on to the bed of the ocean. Gone with all the useful things that she held – pillows, folding chairs, food and first-aid kit. Sunglasses, towels and compass. Now they would never be able to fetch any of them back to shore.

'Monkey!' Mia whimpered.

Fleur kneeled beside her and held her tight. Alfie stared through the mist at the bare rock where *Merlin* had been.

＊

'This has been the worst day so far,' Alfie said with a glum expression.

The rain had cleared and the evening air was calm

when he, Fleur and Mia walked the shoreline.

'Day 7,' Mia added. 'We've been here a whole week.'

Fleur didn't say anything but she felt sure that they'd reached a turning point on Dolphin Island. Yes, *Merlin* had sunk on to the seabed, never to be seen again. Yes, the family had suffered in the storm, but they'd kept the fire going in spite of everything. Their new shelter was still in one piece. Best of all, George had put in an appearance during supper, scampering out of the bushes to feast on jackfruit and coconut.

'I have nightmares after a storm,' Alfie confessed as he stooped and let water trickle between his fingers.

'You never mentioned that before.' Fleur wanted him to look at her but he turned his back.

'I dream I'm drowning and it's so real that it wakes me up. It's horrid.' Waves breaking over his head, swallowing him up, dragging him down.

'You're not really drowning, Alfie.' Mia did her best to forget about losing Monkey for ever and tried to comfort her brother. 'You're with us.'

'That's right. We're in this together.' Rather than dwell on the problems of being stranded on a desert island, you could actually say that things were looking up, Fleur realized. 'Each day we're exploring and finding different things to eat. Dad is getting better.' She stood in the shallow waves and looked out across the smooth surface of the ocean, right out to the horizon where a red sun melted into the golden sea. 'Actually, we're doing fine. And you know people are out there looking for us. We can't see them yet and they can't see us, but they're there.'

Alfie thought it through. 'I guess there are navigation experts who can trace *Merlin*'s course across the Torres Strait. They'll fix our last known position and work out from that where the currents would carry us.' Gazing out across the calm sea he felt a weight of worry slip from his shoulders.

'When?' Mia asked.

'Eventually,' Fleur and Alfie said with determined voices.

They stood side by side, with the sea in front and their beach behind.

'We can explore the forest together,' Fleur reminded Alfie and Mia. 'We'll find fruit and lianas there and lots more wood for the fire. It's exciting.'

'And we can make a mast for the raft then sail it around the island looking for driftwood and coconuts.' Shrugging off his nightmares, Alfie looked to the future with a brave smile.

'When?' This time Mia sounded more hopeful. She liked the idea of exploring the forest and sailing the raft.

'Tomorrow,' Alfie promised.

'Yes – tomorrow,' Fleur agreed.

The sun slipped below the horizon and the sea turned deepest blue. And here, through the calm water, swam their very own pod of dolphins with Pearl at their head, followed by Stormy and Jazz. They were back from deep waters where they'd sheltered from the latest storm, ready to leap and twist in midair, to play with and watch over Mia, Alfie and Fleur Fisher of Dolphin Island.

The story
continues
in ...

Read on for
a sneak peek ...

Chapter One

Alfie Fisher woke in the middle of the night to hear waves crashing on to the shore. They roared in with a rush and a whoosh, drowning out all other sounds.

He lay in the shelter with his eyes wide open, staring up at the canvas roof, waiting patiently for daylight.

On their sleeping mats beside him, his sisters Fleur and Mia were still fast asleep. His dad, James, shifted in his hammock and groaned. His mum, Katie, snored gently.

Alfie remembered what had woken him. It was a bad dream about sailing a small boat into the eye of a mighty storm. The wind howled, the waves rose higher and broke over the deck. He had to hang on to the guardrail for dear life.

Only, it wasn't just a dream, Alfie realized as he lay

in the dark. It had really happened – the tropical storm eight days earlier, the giant waves that had battered their yacht *Merlin* until she'd hit rocks and he'd been tossed overboard. That's how come he was here now with his family, marooned on Dolphin Island. They'd all had to abandon the boat and make for the shore.

A creature scuttled across the floor – light, dry footsteps belonging to something larger than an insect, smaller than a rat. It came and perched on his chest, staring at him with wide lizard eyes.

Alfie's chest rose and fell with his breaths. 'Hello, George,' he whispered to Fleur's pet gecko.

The gecko shot out his long tongue and caught a mosquito.

Are you really George? Alfie wondered. All geckos looked alike to him – small and green and scaly. George was friendlier than the rest due to the fact that Fleur fed him scraps of fruit.

Minutes ticked by but Alfie didn't want to go back to sleep in case the bad dream returned. Instead he counted the insect-bite bumps on his legs and reached twenty-three. Then he planned his day. He would take a swim before breakfast, when hopefully Pearl and the other young dolphins from what he thought of as the Fisher family's special pod would show up. Afterwards he would go beachcombing in the hope of finding useful debris from *Merlin*.

That would be interesting. Who knew what would wash up on to the shore after yesterday's fresh disaster, when *Merlin* had finally broken up on the rocks and sunk without a trace? Maybe more knives from the galley kitchen – they would always come in handy. Foam cushions and mattresses from the cabins would be good too.

He tried to cheer himself up with ideas about what else he could do to make life easier – more coconut-shell cups to drink out of, a fishing rod and line if he found more of the boat's rigging – but his thoughts kept swinging back to the day before and *Merlin's* disappearance below the waves.

More adventures on
Dolphin Island

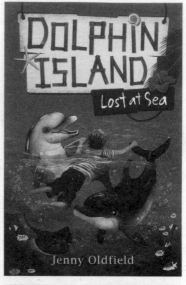

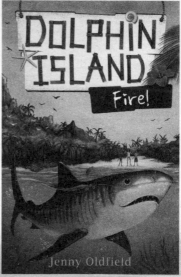

Six books to collect!